P9-AGP-276

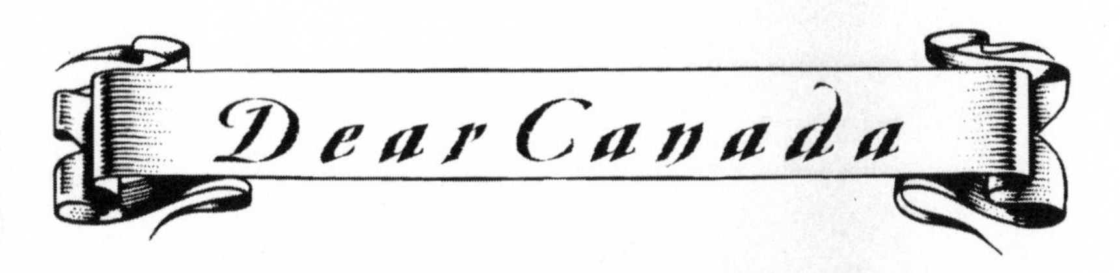

That Fatal Night

The *Titanic* Diary of Dorothy Wilton

BY SARAH ELLIS

Scholastic Canada Ltd.

Halifax, Nova Scotia, 1912

May 1, 1912

Father and Mother met with the principal this morning. I am not allowed to go to school for the rest of the year due to my shocking behaviour yesterday in the schoolyard. I am to do my lessons at home. This afternoon Miss Caughey brought my books to me. She also brought this notebook. She said, "When you are ready, write an account of what happened to you this spring. I think it will help."

All right. I am ready.

My name is Dorothy Pauline Wilton. I am twelve years old. I live in Halifax. I have one brother, Charles, who is grown up and lives in New York City. I was in England visiting Grandfather and Grandmother at their house, Mill House, and I was coming home on a big new ship called the *Titanic* with Miss Pugh, who works in Father's bank but was travelling to England to see her very old father so was taking care of me, and the *Titanic* hit an iceberg and it sank.

Many people drowned. I survived. Miss Pugh did not. Now I'm home.

That is what happened.

Done.

Over.

May 2

When I read over what I wrote yesterday it sounds as though I was cross with Miss Caughey. I was not. She is the kindest teacher in the school. But I am not going to write about the *Titanic* disaster. I am not going to write anything more about it, or talk about it, or think about it. The newspaper man at the train station said, "You're part of history now, kid." I am not. I refuse. I am a schoolgirl, not some old person in history.

But even though I do not want to write about the disaster I am going to write about Wednesday, because it was not fair.

The first thing that I want to say is that I am not one particle sorry. Irene's mother, Mrs. Rudge, says that Irene may never be the same. The principal, Mrs. Trueman, says she would like to be lenient, given my "unusual and troubling recent experience," but that Halifax Ladies' College "simply cannot condone violence of this nature." Mother says that it is "never acceptable for a young lady to behave in such a manner." Aunt Hazel says that this is what comes of giving a child too much attention. Father says I should never have been sent to England and it is all the fault of Grandmother and Grandfather, who are irresponsible bohemians.

Adults know nothing. Bloody nothing. Mother says that "bloody" is vulgar. I don't care. Bloody. Bloody. BLOODY.

May 3

I hear Father and Mother coming home. They were at the Fairview cemetery. Today the victims of the disaster were buried in a special section there.

But not Miss Pugh. Her body was not recovered. Or it could not be identified. Thanks to bloody Irene Rudge I think I know why.

I am to spend my time at home doing lessons, reading "improving" books, learning domestic skills and thinking over my bad behaviour.

Today the lessons were French and Sums.

The domestic work was ironing table napkins. I could not get them to come out perfectly square.

Now I will think over my bad behaviour.

No, I will NOT.

I will think over the bad behaviour of Irene Rudge.

I do not like Irene. She was my friend when we were eight years old. When I was eight I liked her for her curly hair. Eight year olds do not always know what is important in a friend. Later I discovered that she always wants to be the centre of attention and to spread gossip. Sometimes girls want to be her friend, but after a time she is always mean to them.

Phoebe told me that after the disaster — but when I was still not at school — Irene got a lot of attention by telling everyone all about her uncle, who was one of the funeral directors who went out on the *Mackay-Bennett* to recover the bodies from the *Titanic*. But when I came back to school and when I was written up in the newspaper, everyone lost interest in Irene's undertaker uncle.

Irene says that I showed off, but she is bloody wrong. I did not show off. I did not even mention the disaster to anybody except Mary. And Louise and Winnifred and a little bit to Flo, but only when they asked. I did not want to talk about it. I don't want to talk about it, or think about it.

I expected that when I was home and back at school, things could be just as they were when I left in February. But they weren't.

On Tuesday morning Irene came over to me when everyone was skipping, out in the schoolyard before the bell. She said she wanted to show me something around the corner of the building. She was acting friendly. I should have known.

When we got out of sight of the others she started to say the most awful things. She said that some of the bodies of the drowned people could not be identified. If they could not tell who the bodies were, they threw them back into the sea, weighted down with iron bars. She pretended that she was sad about this but she was really filled with glee. Nobody would believe me if I tried to tell them the truth about this. Grown-ups never believe these things.

I did not want to hear this and I should have run away, but it was like I was glued to the spot. Then she said that the reason the people could not be identified was that they had been chewed by sea creatures. This is when I was taken over by anger. I did not decide to slap her across the face. My eyes went blurry and my hand just did it. She stepped backward and tripped and fell against the brick wall and cut her head, and I did not plan that either, but I was glad. I was glad to see her stop looking gleeful. I was glad I hurt her. I am still glad. That is it. That is the truth that I can tell only to these pages.

May 4

Today Father went to St. George's Church for one more funeral. It was for a little boy from the *Titanic*. Nobody claimed or identified this boy. I can't understand this. Does nobody miss him? Even if his whole family drowned, don't they have people at home wondering about them? At dinner Father described the funeral. Six sailors from the *Mackay-Bennett* carried a white casket all covered in flowers.

After dinner Father and I took Borden for a walk. Borden is as daft as he was when I left for England. Father says perhaps he is going to act like a puppy his whole life. Father walks just like Grandfather, with long strides, whacking at weeds with his walking stick.

I miss Grandfather and Grandmother so much. I long to be back at Mill House. Something odd has happened to time. It does not feel like two weeks since I have returned home but just an instant, yet my time at Mill House seems long long ago. And the five days on the *Titanic?* Stretched out like a rubber band.

May 5

Church this morning. I am all ready. Bed made. The stripes on my blankets make it so that I can line them up exactly right. The bedspread is harder because it has tufts that don't make a regular pattern. It takes a lot of tugging. Mother says she is pleasantly surprised by how neat I have become and that Grandmother must have been a good influence. That isn't it at all. At Mill House I had a feather quilt and all I did in the morning was pull it up. Sometimes I didn't even do that if I didn't want to move a sleeping cat. Nobody cared. Grandmother is not the reason that I need to make my bed perfectly. I just need to.

I don't want to go to church. People will look at me. Mother says I have already been excused for two weeks and it is time to "resume the routine." Father says he will bring me straight home after.

He did. Home now.

Mother stayed for the social hour but Father and I didn't. Mother likes to chat but Father doesn't because he says he talks to people all week at work. In the service there were special prayers for the victims of the *Titanic* and for their families. Then there was a prayer of thanks for all those "safely delivered home." When the minister said those words I felt a kind of hum, as though everybody would be staring at me if staring were allowed during prayers.

Then we sang For Those in Peril on the Sea because there are still two ships out at the disaster recovering bodies. It talks about tumult and restless waves and foaming deep, but it doesn't say anything about icebergs. Are there icebergs in the Bible? Probably not because they didn't have icebergs in the Sea of Galilee and those other Bible places.

The Old Testament lesson was all about revenge and smiting. Smiting with a stone and smiting with an instrument of iron and smiting with a piece of wood. *Smite* is a word that sounds just like what it is, like a slap across the face.

The improving book that I'm reading is *Madame How and Lady Why*, a book about science and the Earth. The chapter was about earthquakes. The Madame How part was about steam beneath the Earth. I already knew a bit about what is under the ground because of the *Encyclopaedia Britannica.*

Just before I arrived in England Grandfather had bought the *Encyclopaedia Britannica.* (I like spelling *Encyclopaedia.* Perhaps some day it will be on a spelling bee and it will be my winning word.) It was very grand. Twenty-seven books. Black leather covers with gold decorations. Paper so thin you could almost see through it. It even had its own bookcase with twenty-seven slots so that books could all slide in sideways. Each book was from something to something, like FRA to GIB. Millie and I made up creatures for all the three-letter names. BIS and CAL, MUN and ODD, EVA and FRA. VET and ZYM.

I loved the thought that EVERYTHING you could know was sitting on those two shelves. Sometimes Grandfather and I would just pick a volume at random and flip through until we found something we wanted to know about. One day we were flipping through one of the G books and, buried in the middle of *Geology* we found out that there are three ideas about what's in the centre of the Earth. It could be rocks that are so hot they are liquid. It could be solid with just little pockets of red-hot rock. It could be gas with melted rock around that and the solid Earth around that. I asked Grandfather if we would ever find out for sure and he said he thought some clever chap would sort it out one day. Then Grandmother called out from the other room that **it might well be a clever lass.**

(I wrote that in fat letters because Grandmother speaks like that. She has many opinions about government, food, clothes, home decorating, education, the poor and, most especially, women. I won't write them out now.)

On the subject of the encyclopaedia, Grandmother said that they could have better used the money to fix the roof, but then Grandfather said that if the roof leaked he would just read them a nice dry article such as the four pages on land registration.

Back to now, and my improving book. The Madame How part was followed by Lady Why and she just makes me angry. Mr. Kingsley, who wrote the book, asked why did God allow a lot of people to be killed in an earthquake in South America. Then he pretended to have an answer. It was something about tempting God's will. But if it was a punishment for doing something wrong, and he doesn't say what was the wrong thing, how can it include everybody, like mothers and children and that little boy that nobody claimed? I think Mr. Kingsley should stick to steam and not ask questions that he cannot answer.

May 6

Nobody understands. Last night I woke up in the darkness. I wake up at night now. I didn't use to. I reached over the edge of the bed to touch my shoes and they were not there. I got out of bed and felt all around the floor and I could not find them anywhere. This blackness came over me and I heard myself screaming out. Mother came and all I could say was, "Shoes." Finally she went to the wardrobe and got out my shoes. She had put them away when I was asleep. I need to be able to touch my shoes in the night. I cannot tell her why. I can't tell anybody why. Not even in these pages.

Mother was not cross. She stayed with me until I fell asleep.

Phoebe came to visit after school. She reported that Irene is making the most of her injury, wearing a bright white bandage, sitting on the sidelines during Calisthenics ("Wish you'd slugged *me*," Phoebe said. She loathes Calisthenics and sports of all kinds.) and pretending to feel dizzy several times a day. Phoebe says everybody is more than tired of Irene and misses me. I know this can't be true (Irene has her loyal followers) but I'm glad Phoebe said it.

Phoebe admired my new clothes. I have a new coat and boots, hat, three new dresses, underwaists and drawers, nightgowns and combinations. If somebody had told me, before the *Titanic,* that one day I would go with Mother and buy all new clothes, from drawers right out to my coat, I would have thought that would be the best fun. Mother is always very sparkly when she is shopping, like someone at a party. But that is what happened the first week I was home and it wasn't fun. Every new thing made me think of something lost, something drowned. I tried to be grateful and good but I could not be cheerful. Nobody understands.

May 7

Today there was a package of letters for me from England. When I opened the package and all the letters spilled out I could see a picture in my mind of everyone at Mill House.

Grandfather in his chair, reading and trying to keep his pipe lit. Grandmother on a ladder painting a scene on the wall above the fireplace. Mrs. Hawkins in the kitchen kneading bread dough. Owen Hawkins under the kitchen table teaching Brownie to balance a biscuit on her nose. Millie Hawkins doing the splits.

The longest letter was from Grandfather. He told me the whole story of how they first heard of the disaster in the newspaper and how all the news was muddled and how desperate they had been until they received Father's telegram. He wrote that he kept saying to himself, "But it's unsinkable."

When I opened the note from Mrs. Hawkins, dried flowers sprinkled out. She wrote that she missed me and that the chickens missed me too and were not laying well. She wondered if I remembered the names of the flowers. I do. Bluebell, coltsfoot, butterbur, primrose.

Owen, whose penmanship is execrable (good word for *bad)*, told me that he had the stitches taken out of his arm and it looks as though there is going to be a very good scar and did I see the iceberg and was it as big as the crurcr or not so big. I puzzled over that for a while, wondering if a "crurcr" was some English thing I didn't know about. Then I sorted it out. Church.

Millie sent a drawing of the encyclopaedia creatures, CHA and SHU and LOR and all the rest. Millie's drawings are like the ones in a book that Grandfather had, called *Book of Nonsense.* I wish I had that book. In her envelope there was also a scrap of paper with a muddy footprint on it, a shake-a-paw from Brownie to Borden.

I saved Grandmother's letter for last. She wrote that she has started to knit me a new cardigan. She has made a dye of ragweed buds and she says it has turned out to be a beautiful green.

When I read this I cried. For my dark red cardigan that Grandmother made. For my locket that I got on my twelfth birthday. For my book of *The Railway Children* that Mrs. Bland gave me. For the plum pudding from Mrs. Hawkins that was going to be just perfect by Christmas. I know that people lost people in their families in the disaster. I know that old Mr. Pugh in England lost his daughter and that Marjorie, my best *Titanic* friend, lost her father, and that some family — and we don't even know who they are — lost their little boy. I know that I should not cry over just *things*. But I did.

May 8

As of today I am a prisoner.

I completed my lessons before lunch. The truth is that it is much quicker to do lessons at home than at school. But I do miss school. I am missing the choir concert. Before I left I was getting much better at basketball and now that I'm a whole inch taller I'm probably even better. Most of all I miss my friends. I had so much to tell them and I did not get a chance. And now, because of what happened this afternoon, I probably won't.

After lunch Mother said we should leave lessons and domestic tasks and go for a walk because spring was in the air. We walked to Point Pleasant Park. Usually my favourite thing to do in the park is scramble out on the rocks, but I did not want to. I did not even want to look out at the waves. So we walked in the forest instead.

Mother did not mention my bad behaviour but instead talked about things like the church fete and Aunt Hazel's sciatica and Charles shaving off his moustache, and what a shame it was that Mr. Amundsen beat Mr. Scott to the South Pole. The only correcting thing she said was that I had grown taller since I was in England and that she hoped I would not grow too tall but that in any case I must be careful not to slouch because she had noticed that the Potters' oldest girl had shot up like a beanpole and was slouching and how that was very unattractive and a bad habit and easily cured by pretending that you have a string coming out the top of your head.

When Mother talks you don't really need to reply. You can just say "hmm" every so often. Father and Charles tease her and call her "the gramophone," but today I liked it. It was ordinary.

On the way home we walked up Young Ave. and when we got almost to Inglis there was a small crowd gathered. Two men with cameras were taking pictures of the house at 989 Young, which is a fancy, fairy-tale kind of house with a round tower. Mother told me that it was the house of George Wright. I knew who he was. They wrote about him in the newspaper. He was a wealthy businessman and he was on the *Titanic*. In the newspaper he was a four-words: "*Titanic* Tragedy: Halifax Businessman." I was a four-words too. "Local Schoolgirl: *Titanic* Survivor."

We stopped and joined the crowd. Someone said that the photographers were from an illustrated paper. People were talking about what a good man Mr. Wright was, and how when he wasn't being a businessman he lectured on intemperance and immorality and tried to inspire people to be better. Then the conversation got a bit gossipy and people said that he had no wife and family and they wondered who he had left his fortune to.

We were just turning to go when one of the photographers suddenly said, "Hold on! Isn't that Dorothy Wilton from the *Titanic?*" And then someone else said, "Yes, it is!"

Then everyone turned to me. Mother said, "Come along," and took my arm and we started to walk away, but the crowd swarmed around us and one of the photographers tried to take my picture. One called out, "Did you meet George Wright on board?" There was no real reason to feel frightened, but I did. Frightened and trapped. Mother gripped my arm more securely and said quietly, "Just keep moving," and we walked away. I felt like running but Mother moved like a ship pulling away from the dock and the people parted as she sailed through them.

We kept sailing, right to Father's bank, where we went to his office and his secretary brought us cups of tea. Then Father made one of the young men walk us home. By this time I was over my fright and it seemed silly to have to have skinny Mr. Nevin guard us as we went home.

But now Mother and Father have decided that I must not go out on my own but only with them or Cook or another adult.

I think about my days in Lewisham, going on expeditions on my own, getting lost, being a musketeer. I only had to be back in time for tea. I wish I could wind the clock backwards.

Second wish: that Charles were here. He could have been another adult. I know he had to go back to his job in New York, but to be a prisoner and an only child as well is hateful.

Did I see Mr. Wright? I do wonder if he might have been the man with the pointy moustache who was at Marjorie's table. But I am not going to write about that.

There is something else about our visit to the bank. When we went through the outer office I saw the desk where Miss Pugh used to sit. It was bare. If only. If only Miss Pugh had not worked in Father's bank. If only she had not been going to England to visit her father. If only Father had not asked her to take care of me on the voyage. If only there had not been an iceberg. If only there had been more lifeboats. If only I was never taken over by a temper. There is no end to if only.

May 9

Miss Caughey brought over more school work today and commented on how quickly I'm getting on in Math. She is different than she is in school, not so brisk. She brought me a poem that she had copied out.

It is called "The Jumblies." She said that it was the cheeriest poem that she knew and a very good one to carry around in your head. Then she said it was written by a man called Edward Lear and I know about him because he's the same person who wrote the nonsense book that Grandfather had at Mill House. Miss Caughey knew about it too. She even knew some of the poems by heart, like the one about the young lady whose chin resembled the point of a pin. She said she would bring me her own copy.

I am to memorize "The Jumblies." That is hardly like school work.

She asked me if I am writing in the notebook and I said I was. Which is true. She did not ask me if I was writing about the disaster. Which I am not.

May 10

Today I have decided that I am going to wind the clock backwards. I am going to write about what happened, but not what happened on that horrible night, just what happened in England.

But first, school work.

THEY went to sea in a sieve, they did;
In a sieve they went to sea;
In spite of all their friends could say,
On a winter's morn, on a stormy day,
In a sieve they went to sea.
And when the sieve turn'd round and round,
And every one cried, "You'll all be drown'd!"
They call'd aloud, "Our sieve ain't big:
But we don't care a button; we don't care a fig:
In a sieve we'll go to sea!"
Far and few, far and few,
Are the lands where the Jumblies live:

Their heads are green, and their hands are blue;
And they went to sea in a sieve.

Just writing out the first verse in good handwriting, I know it almost by heart. This will be an easy task.

May 11

Now that I am home, England seems like a play, a play that I was in, day and night, for two months.

The reason that I know about plays is that Grandfather and Grandmother put on plays in their house. Their friends come to visit and they all dress up in costumes and push the furniture around to make the places in the play. The first Saturday I was there they put on *A Midsummer Night's Dream* and I got to play the part of a fairy called Cobweb who has four things to say: "And I." "Hail." "Cobweb." and "Ready."

I'm getting ahead of myself. Before I describe that little play I am going to introduce the big play which is called *A Canadian Girl in England.* You have already met some of the *dramatis personae* (that's characters). They are Grandfather and Grandmother (their real names are Henry Wilton and Augusta Wilton), Mrs. Hawkins (who takes care of the house), Owen Hawkins (age 12, her son), Millie Hawkins (age 12, her daughter), Fabian and Bernard (the inside cats), and Brownie (the dog). Other characters in the play are Mrs. Bland (a book writer), the Rev. Drysdale (a vicar), and many chickens and more adults without names. Oh yes, and a Canadian girl, the daughter of Mr. Stanley Wilton who is the son of Mr. and Mrs. Henry Wilton. This character will be called The Canadian Girl or the CG.

The play takes place in a house called Mill House near a village called Lewisham in the county of London in the country of England where The Canadian Girl is staying because her grandparents wanted to get to know her and because her older brother, Charles (23 years old and acts like a man), had the same opportunity when he was a boy, and **girls should have all the opportunities that boys have.**

What kind of a play is it? Is it a mystery or a thriller or the sort of play in which people sit at dinner and say clever things? Does it have beautiful costumes? Does it have music and dancing? Do people jump down from walls and fight with swords? Does one of the characters turn out to be somebody else?

Yes.

Oh bother. It is lunchtime. Already? I have not done any lessons.

Try Sums or Jumblies? I choose Jumblies. It is

such a good poem that when I write it out it goes directly from my fingers into my head.

They sail'd away in a sieve, they did,
In a sieve they sail'd so fast,
With only a beautiful pea-green veil
Tied with a ribbon, by way of a sail,
To a small tobacco-pipe mast.
And every one said who saw them go,
"Oh! won't they be soon upset, you know:
For the sky is dark, and the voyage is long;
And, happen what may, it's extremely wrong
In a sieve to sail so fast."

May 12

The play begins when The Canadian Girl wakes up in a little whitewashed attic room where the ceiling slopes down to the floor. Brownie is lying across her feet. (The grandmother of The Canadian Girl told her the night before that she might have the dog to sleep in her room in case she was homesick. The Canadian Girl's mother, who would never let Borden upstairs, would have been fit to be tied to have a dog in a bedroom, but The Canadian Girl liked it very much, even though she was too tired to be homesick. When she did wake up she loved the weight of the dog and hearing it breathe.)

You might wonder why the play does not start earlier. What about the ocean voyage? What about the train to Lewisham? What about meeting her grandparents for the first time? I have one word to tell you:

SEASICK

I was so sick on the voyage to England that sometimes I thought the whole world had disappeared and all that was left was up, up, up . . . (horrible pause) . . . down. The stewardess tried everything. Ginger beer. Salty crackers. Mint tea. Parsley to chew. Even Mothersill's Seasick Remedy. She also tried singing to me to take my mind off my stomach. But nothing worked except that now I don't care for ginger, crackers, mint, parsley or "Let Me Call You Sweetheart."

(I see that The Canadian Girl has become "I." But you knew that already. Not like in a very good book called *The Story of the Treasure Seekers,* where the person who is telling the story is Oswald but he pretends it isn't and you don't figure out for quite a while that "I" is Oswald although when you look back later you see that "I" praises everything about Oswald. Well, Owen said he figured it out in chapter one but I think he was just bragging.)

So back to the play and the CG.

Act one. Scene one. Whitewashed bedroom. The curtain rises and the CG is woken up by voices yelling: One for all and all for one.

The CG, *gets up and looks out the window. There is a garden like a room, with brick walls. Rain is dripping off the trees but there is a little weak sunshine. Suddenly, enter two hats at the top of the wall, black hats with red feathers. Then two heads under the hats, then two bodies under the heads. With swords and capes. Then the two bodies jump off the wall with their capes billowing out behind them and they run across the lawn, holding their swords above their heads.*

The two characters: All for one and one for all.

(They say this sort of by themselves and sort of together. Hard to explain but easy to understand.)

As they disappear inside, the CG notices two things. One is that the floor and the windowsill are not going up, up, up, and (horrible pause) down, but just staying in one lovely, heavenly, glorious, still place. The other is that she is so hungry that she could eat a moose.

Oh. Play.

The CG, *to Brownie the dog:* I'm so hungry that I could eat a moose.
Brownie: Woof.

(The CG didn't really say that she could eat a moose but she thought it. The CG does not think she can stand to wait to get washed and dressed and eat breakfast and to find out about the cape people. And she doesn't have to.)

Enter, **Grandmother:** Just come down to the kitchen in your nightgown and robe, Dorothy. The porridge is ready and waiting.

(The CG's Mother would never let the CG eat in the kitchen OR wear her nightgown to breakfast.)

The CG: This is like all the good parts of being sick without the being sick to spoil it.

(The CG didn't really say this out loud either. And the CG's mother isn't even in the *dramatis personae.* It is quite hard to write a play. I'm going to start again tomorrow.)

May 13

Act one. Scene two. A very tidy kitchen. A woman is standing at the stove stirring a pot.

The two cape people are sitting at the table without their hats.

The CG: This kitchen smells delicious.

Grandmother: Dorothy, this is Mrs. Hawkins.

Mrs. Hawkins: Welcome to Mill House, Dorothy. We've been looking forward to this for ages. That's Owen. That's Millie. They are my barbarian children. They've already eaten but they don't want to miss any time with you. They've been looking forward to the Canadian for months. Don't let them talk your ear off before you've had your breakfast. Here's your tea. Do you take sugar with it? *(Mrs. Hawkins's voice has a smile in it.)*

Millie: We're not really Owen and Millie.

Not-Owen: I am Athos.

Not-Millie: I am Porthos. We've been waiting for you so you can be . . .

Not-Millie and Not-Owen together: Aramis.

(The CG does not know what they are talking about but she doesn't care because of the porridge. At that moment it is the best thing the CG has ever tasted. She did not stop to say, "This is the best thing I have ever tasted," because she was so busy eating. In the play the actress playing the CG will have to look very happy. It was the thick kind, with little chewy bits that just make your teeth happy. There was thick yellow cream in a blue and white striped jug and brown sugar. The CG has two bowls full and then a small bit extra, not because she is hungry but just because her mouth wanted it.)

The CG: This is so much better than moose.
Brownie, *who is the only one who understands what she is talking about:* Woof.

(The cape people sit like dogs who have been told to "stay" and are just waiting for the word.)

The CG, *puts down her spoon.*
Mrs. Hawkins: All right then. Now you can talk.

Millie and Owen are twins and they have a way of talking which is hard to describe and tiresome to write in a play, but easy to understand. It is like they share the sentence, each saying one part of it. Later Mrs. Hawkins tells the CG that when they were wee ones they had their own language. That first morning the CG cannot figure out if they felt younger or older than her. In Halifax twelve years old is much too old to be playing with swords and costumes, so in that way they seemed young, but the CG doesn't know if that is just because they are English. But then they tell the CG all about the story of The Three Musketeers, which they had read in French. Their French is much better than the CG's and in that way they seemed older. They had also read some adventure books set in Canada.

Twins: Do you know how to make a birchbark canoe?
The CG: No.
Twins: Dry whortleberries?
The CG: No.
Twins: Build a log cabin?
The CG: No.
Twins: Make a broom out of cedar boughs bound together with a leathern thong?
The CG: No.
Twins: Make a bowstring out of the entrails of a woodchuck?
The CG: No.
Twins: What DO you do?
The CG: I can crochet. I can make jam, with help. I go to school. We learn Geography and French and Elocution and Calisthenics. I might be on the basketball team next year.
Twins: Oh.

(This conversation and three bowls of porridge — that sounds like Goldilocks and the Three Bears —

lasts until midmorning and the CG is still in her nightgown.)

The CG: I can see that life at Mill House is going to be different from life at home.

(Of course she doesn't really say this. Nobody would say such a thing, but they might *think* it and she did.)

CURTAIN.

May 14

Programme Notes! I've just remembered how you can put things into a play that everybody needs to know but you can't get somebody to say or act out. The plays at Mill House always had a programme with notes.

Programme Notes for A *Canadian Girl in England.*

(You can't understand this play unless you know about The Three Musketeers.)

There is a fellow called D'Artagnan but he isn't one of The Three Musketeers. (In this play D'Artagnan, when he is needed, is played by Brownie the dog, who also plays many other roles.) The real three musketeers are Porthos, Athos and Aramis and they are D'Artagnan's friends. D'Artagnan gets into lots of trouble, mostly because he is in love with Constance who is married to somebody else. The Three Musketeers help him out. For example, The Three Musketeers have to rescue Constance who is kidnapped by Cardinal Richelieu, who is hired by the King of France to keep an eye on his wife, the Queen, who is also in love with somebody else and has given him the jewels that her husband gave to her and now she needs them back so the King doesn't find out about it.

This is too hard. *The Three Musketeers* is a very long, complicated book.

This is what you really need to know:

1. One of the characters is usually in prison. We set up a jail in the back of the small stone barn with an old rusty bedstead. Whoever was in jail lived on bread and water from a tin cup.
2. When we needed to have women, Millie was Constance and I was Milady De Winter, which meant that I got to have a *fleur-de-lys* (the mark of a criminal) drawn onto my shoulder with pen and ink.
3. Many people are murdered. Sometimes they are mown down in sword fights. Sometimes they are knifed. (You just slide the knife in under the arm and it looks very real.) Sometimes they get their heads chopped off. They best thing is when they are poi-

soned, like Constance. (Millie sip-sip-sips from the jewelled goblet that Milady gives her and then falls on the ground, or the floor if it was too wet outside, writhing, in the arms of her beloved D'Artagnan — played by Brownie.)

May 15

Scene: The garden. The Three Musketeers lie in wait on top of the garden wall.
Enter, **an agent of Cardinal Richelieu.** *He walks by, unsuspecting.*
Athos: For King and Cardinal!
Porthos: We brook no insult!
Aramis: Prepare to die! *(With a roar the musketeers leap off the wall, their capes rippling behind them, their swords held high. They stick a knife in the agent.)*
Agent: *(death gurgle)*
The Three Ms: We live to fight again!
(In this performance the role of the agent is played by a barn cat.)

This scene could not have happened in Halifax. In Halifax I am a young lady (who does not slouch). But in Lewisham I am Aramis. In Halifax twelve years old is much too old to be playing such games, but in Lewisham twelve is different.

In the evenings or if it was really too rainy out we did a different play, inside. It was called *Lost in the Bush in Canada.* Millie hid under the bearskin rug and pretended to attack Owen and me. It wasn't as good a play as The Musketeers.

A few days before I left to come home we acted out the wall-jumping scene one more time. The thought of me leaving made us all wilder than usual and somehow Owen tripped as he sailed off the wall and he ended up ripping his arm open on his broken sword. There was a lot of blood. But he was very brave and said that it had always been his heart's desire to have a manly scar.

I was glad to know from Grandfather's letter that Owen got his scar. The mark of a valiant musketeer.

May 16

Miss Caughey came again today. She remembered to bring me the nonsense poem book. I recited the first two verses of "The Jumblies" and she joined in on "Far and few." Then she remembered that she was a teacher and we did some Geography. When I showed her how many pages I had written in this notebook she was very impressed. She flipped through without reading and complimented me on its neatness. What she doesn't know is that I'm not as neat as it looks. Sometimes I make splotches and then I have to

Never mind about that. I don't care a button. I don't care a fig.

After she left I looked at all the drawings in the nonsense book. They made me feel I was back in the parlour at Mill House. The Young Lady whose bonnet came untied when the birds sat upon it is my favourite person and my favourite drawing. She is balancing on one tiptoe and smiling as an owl and a crow and some other birds sit on her hat and a flock of other birds come toward her. When I was little there was an old man who used to sit on the bench outside the church and put birdseed on his hat to make the birds come. Mother never let me talk to him.

I am sorry that I ever once complained about school. It is boring without school. Adults don't understand about being bored. They say, "There is always something to do," and then they suggest some kind of *chore*. But being bored is because there is nothing to do that you *want* to do. It is like being hungry. "How can you be hungry? You didn't finish your Brussels sprouts." Have they forgotten that you can be hungry for currant bread and butter or marmalade roly-poly at the same time that you are not hungry for Brussels sprouts?

Miss Caughey suggested that since I like Mr. Lear's poems so much I might try to write one myself.

There was a young lady from Halifax.

There was a young lady called Dorothy.

That's no good. Nothing rhymes with Halifax or Dorothy.

May 17

Success.

There was a young gal named Miss Wilton
Who lived upon nothing but Stilton.

Stilton is a cheese that Grandfather likes. Very stinky. A bad English food idea. The Jumblies also buy Stilton when they get to the Western Sea.

And they bought an owl, and a useful cart,
And a pound of rice, and a cranberry tart,
And a hive of silvery bees:
And they bought a pig, and some green jackdaws,
And a lovely monkey with lollipop paws,
And seventeen bags of edelweisss tea,
And forty bottles of ring-bo-ree,
And no end of Stilton cheese.

But I still cannot think of another rhyme for *Wilton.*

May 18

I was never bored at Mill House. One of the promises that Grandfather made Father was that I would keep up with my lessons. I thought that would mean that I would have to sit with my school books every day and do Sums and Penmanship, but the second morning (when I did not sleep in and eat porridge in my nightgown), Grandfather handed me the newspaper and that began a new kind of lessons.

Scene: Dining room at Mill House. Morning. Grandfather, Grandmother, Canadian Girl.

Props: Brownie, Fabian, Bernard.

(The CG *has finished her porridge. Grandfather is eating scrambled eggs and kidneys.* (Another very bad English food idea.) *Grandmother is drinking coffee.* ("Cannot abide breakfast.")

Grandfather, *hands newspaper to* CG: There you go. Find something that interests you and we'll discuss it.

The CG, *tries to read the newspaper but the front page is all adverts and she can't seem to turn it to the second page and fold it up neatly the way Grandfather does with that neat little snap. A corner of the newspaper falls into the marmalade.*

The CG: Can I spread it out on the floor?

Grandmother: Oh, of course. The only sensible way to read the paper.
The CG, *lies on her stomach and looks through the paper:* Price of rubber? Coal strike?
Grandfather: Do you find those interesting topics?
The CG: Not really.
Grandfather: Then look further.
The CG: What's vi-vi-section?
Grandmother: Oh Hal, I don't think Dorothy needs to know about that. **Not approprate for a twelve year old.**
Grandfather: On the contrary. An excellent topic for discussion and a rich lesson for today. *(Clears his throat.)* Vivisection is testing scientific things using animals. You read the article and tell me what you think.

(Grandfather said this in a grander way, but this is what I remember.)

The CG, *reads:* It says that some people think it is wrong, but it doesn't say why.
Grandfather: The main objection is that sometimes the subjects are still alive when they test them.
The CG: You mean when they cut into

them? *(Reaches over and covers Brownie's ears.)* That's cruel!

Grandfather: A strong conviction against something is a good place to start a discussion. Your position is shared by many famous people, including the late Queen Victoria and our friend Mr. Wells. He has written a whole novel against vivisection. Perhaps reading that could be an assignment.

Grandmother: Absolutely not, Hal! Dorothy is welcome to read it if she likes, as she is welcome to read any book we have, but you are NOT to assign it. It is a very sad and worrying book.

The CG: So I got the right answer? Is that it for lessons for today?

Grandfather, *fills his teacup:* Not quite. Let's make the question more complicated. How do you know that animals suffer? How do you know that animals feel pain the way we do, as they can't talk? No, don't answer. That's your question for the day. Think about it. That's enough school.

Grandmother: I should say so. Off you go.

CURTAIN.

May 19

Asquith is sitting on my lap, kneading my leg. When I first came home he was standoffish but now he has forgiven me for going away and demands attention, butting my hand if I forget to scratch him under the chin. He is saying, "Petting me is your job and don't forget that for a minute." The fact that Asquith can talk reminds me that the vivisection discussion and lesson went on for about a week's worth of breakfasts.

Breakfast scene: As before, more kidneys.
The CG: Animals can talk, they just don't use words like we do.
Grandfather: Good point. Give me an example.
The CG: Asquith our cat can talk. If we put anything new on the mantle at home, Asquith jumps up and knocks it off saying, "This is my mantle and I don't want you to change anything about it." And also, we know that animals are in pain because they cry or yelp, like the time I accidentally stepped on Borden our puppy when Phoebe and I were pretending to be blind.

(The idea of crying reminds the CG of another good argument.)

The CG: Anyway, what about babies? Babies don't talk but we know they feel pain.

Grandfather, *claps his hands:* Bravo, good baby argument.

The CG: So is the lesson over?

Grandfather: Not quite. Some scientists use animal testing so they can discover things to help sick people. For example, they use guinea pigs to find out about diphtheria. Their discoveries could save thousands of lives. In fact, they might get rid of diphtheria altogether. But some of the guinea pigs die. Is it worth it if one guinea pig saves one human? What if one guinea pig saves a thousand humans? Think about it for tomorrow.

CURTAIN.

May 20

The Play now has a name: SCENES AT BREAKFAST.

Scene: Still the same except Grandfather switches to bacon.

(The guinea-pig question was hard because Phoebe used to have a guinea pig and she was lovely. She was black and brown and white and was called Zanzibar and we would take her cage out onto the lawn in the summer and take the bottom out so she could nibble grass. She made the dearest noise, like a bubbling whistle, and she was very fond of cucumber. I could not bear to think of her being hurt.)

The CG: Scientists just have to find a way of solving diphtheria without murdering guinea pigs.
Grandfather: Excellent! You have taken a position and defended it with vigour.
The CG, *hopefully:* So tomorrow can we talk about the price of rubber?
Grandfather: There is just one more thing.
The CG, *moans.*
Grandmother: Hal, show the child some mercy.
Grandfather: She doesn't need mercy. She is up to the challenge. What about if the experiments were not on guinea pigs but on rats or frogs or worms? Think about it and away you go.

Mother has just called me. Some ladies are coming for tea and I'm supposed to help set out the cakes.

May 21

I have asked Father to get me a new notebook. I am almost at the end of this one. I am going through the pages quickly because if I make an ink splotch I tear out the page and start over. I know this is wasteful. One day I tried leaving the splotch, telling myself that it didn't matter because nobody will read this notebook and I just went on writing, but I couldn't bear it so I got up in the night and tore the page out and then I had to re-copy the next few pages. I just can't carry on and leave a mess behind. It doesn't feel good.

The tea was dull. I passed the cream and sugar and was well-behaved. The ladies were discussing hatpins. Did you know that most hatpins are too long and need to be filed off to the correct length? I wonder what would have happened if I had asked what all the ladies thought of vivisection?

VIVISECTION: **The Next Scene**

(In between the last scene and this, the CG has been weeding the perennial beds and reading Grandmother's old Girl's Own Annuals and playing bow-and-arrow target practice with Millie and Owen and has not thought very much about worms.)

The CG: Worms would be fine if it meant that many babies could be saved from diphtheria.

Grandfather: But what is the difference between guinea pigs and worms?
The CG, *knows that this argument won't work but she tries it anyway:* Guinea pigs are pretty and friendly and worms are just worms.
Grandfather: So animals that are pretty and friendly are worth more than animals that are ugly and grumpy? Does that apply to people? Are good-looking people (I could use myself as an example in this respect) . . .
Grandmother:

(A sound where she makes a little explosion come out of her mouth but I don't know how to write that.)

Grandfather: If I could just continue without audience heckling. Are good-looking and friendly people worth more than hideous grumps?

CURTAIN.

And it was all complicated again.

May 22

VIVISECTION: **The Final Scene**

(Thank Goodness for that!)

Mill House, breakfast table, rain pattering on windows.

(I don't really remember if it was raining but I thought the scene needed a bit more description. It was probably raining. It seemed to rain part of almost every day at Mill House.)

Brownie, *lying on floor under table, ever hopeful of falling scraps.*
Props: porridge, kidneys, cats, etc. etc.
The CG: I am stumped. I still don't want guinea pigs to be hurt but I sometimes cut worms in half by mistake when I'm digging in the garden and that doesn't even save anyone from diphtheria but it doesn't make me feel too bad, and slapping mosquitoes I don't care about one bit. So I give up.
Grandfather: Top marks! Very well done, Dorothy!
The CG: ?
Grandfather: You have discovered that you can hold a strong position even if it is inconsistent. Remember, "A foolish consistency is the hobgoblin of little minds." Somebody clever said that.
Grandmother: Does this mean that our daily discussion of vivisection is over?

The CG: Yes, please.
Grandmother: Thank heavens.

CURTAIN.

Grandmother wasn't the only one who was happy that topic was over. The difference between guinea pigs and worms was starting to make me feel as though I had hobgoblins in my head. I have remembered Grandfather's quotation though, hoping I would get a chance to use it on somebody, say, like Irene Rudge, but I probably won't get a chance because now she will never talk to me again.

May 23

You might think that all I did at Mill House was eat breakfast and discuss vivisection. But every day was full. For one thing there were some other lessons. Mrs. Hawkins did not hold with learning with the newspaper so she set me Sums, but not every day. Of course she sent Millie and Owen to school and they were jealous as can be. With the work that Miss Caughey brings me home I don't seem too far behind.

Then there was gathering eggs and tending to the rabbits and digging in the garden. There was cutting out scones for Mrs. Hawkins. There was exploring, inside and out.

There were The Three Musketeers with murders and hangings and poisonings and swords to be repaired.

There was Grandfather's fossil collection (I pretended to be learning Science with them but really I just liked arranging families. The Trilobite Family: mother, father and the baby Bites. The Ammonites: Mister, Missus, Auntie and the seven children.) There was an ongoing jigsaw puzzle on a table in the parlour and there was always somebody willing to play ludo or checkers.

I also spent a lot of time playing the piano. Somebody forgot to tell them that I was supposed to practise the piano, so I didn't play one scale while I was there. Instead I played my favourite way, which is all on the black keys with the pedal down. The black keys always sound good and a bit mysterious. When I play on the black keys I can imagine myself riding across the moors on a coal-black horse, with my flaxen hair streaming out behind me (when I play the black keys my hair magically becomes long and flaxen), wrapped in a shawl. I ride like the wind and the black keys gallop beneath me. At Mill House nobody minded how long my black-key rides went on. Grandmother even told me that playing on the black keys is called the "pentatonic scale." So I guess I like the C scale, which has no sharps and flats, and the pentatonic scale, which is nothing but sharps and flats. It is the scales in between that are tiresome.

What else went on at Mill House? There was reading, at all times of the day and in all different places. Mill House was messy with reading. There were always newspapers and illustrated papers lying about and books lying on chairs. Sometimes two people would be reading the same book and there was a great to-do when somebody took it away. There were leaves and pencils and crochet hooks stuck in as bookmarks. Once there was a shoelace. There was even a book in the WC! It was called *The Blue Fairy Book.* While I was at Mill House I read all the stories in that book. You would think they would be about fairies but mostly they weren't. Some were tricky and some were peculiar and some were really scary. The scariest one was about a man with a blue beard (which should have been funny — think of the Jumblies with their green heads and blue hands — but wasn't, because he kept chopping his wives' heads off).

Mill House was also messy with talk. Some days it was like a train station, with so many people dropping by. People from the village, friends of G&G, relatives, and all of them liked to talk. At home grown-up talk seems to come in little packages like "What you say when the Vicar comes to tea" or "Father and Charles discuss politics," but at Mill House talk bounced around, hopping from one thing to another, getting lost, being found again, making people cross or making them laugh. The odd time I was alone in the parlour I felt as though the talk was still echoing, or floating down like dust to settle on the settee and the piano.

May 24

I blotched this page once and recopied it and now I've just blotched it again but I'm NOT going to copy it out again.

May 25

Phoebe came over today. We played jacks and she told me that Irene told Leah that she was "too plain to be pretty and too pretty to be plain" and then when Leah's feelings were hurt she said she meant it as a compliment. Then Phoebe said did I want to go down to the Old Market but Mother said I wasn't allowed to go without an adult and she didn't have time to come with us. So we played a bit more, but I was just having trouble being cheery and when Phoebe sat on the bed she messed it up and I just couldn't help my brain from thinking about how soon would she go so that I could tidy it up, even though I didn't want her to go.

I am grumpy. I want to jump out of my skin and run away to the Hills of the Chankly Bore, which is where the Jumblies visit.

May 26

I don't like the way I am. I don't like waking up in the night, afraid, but I can't even remember what was going on in my dream. I don't like the feeling of being outside myself. I'm talking to Phoebe or Mother or Asquith and all of a sudden I'm in some other corner of the room looking at myself. This is not a very good description. I know I'm supposed to be writing about what happened on the *Titanic* but I don't know how to start. I know Miss Caughey believes that writing about it will help me, but she's wrong.

But she's right about "The Jumblies" being cheerful. When I cannot go back to sleep at night I say the poem over and over.

The water it soon came in, it did;
The water it soon came in.
So, to keep them dry, they wrapped their feet
In a pinky paper all folded neat;
And they fastened it down with a pin.
And they passed the night in a crockery-jar;
And each of them said, "How wise we are!

Though the sky be dark, and the voyage be long,
Yet we never can think we were rash or wrong,
While round in our sieve we spin."

Sometimes my mind just says "pinky paper all folded neat" over and over again.

May 27

Mother has a new hat. The milliner brought it around this morning. Hats have their own language, just like ships. Mother and the milliner said things like, "blue and green mixed fancy felt braid, low crown, speckled quill, Chantilly lace and a *cabochon* which provides a touch of completion." Mother told the milliner that it looked so airy that a slight breeze would blow it away and the milliner said that was the nicest thing anyone could say about a hat.

Grandmother didn't usually wear a hat. When we first went out for a walk to the village I thought she had forgotten, so I reminded her and she said, "Oh, I don't favour hats. I like to feel the sun on my head and the wind in my hair." That was very hard to get used to. I don't believe I have ever seen a grown woman on the street in Halifax without a hat. Grandmother did wear a hat to church, but it was a very plain brown-felt one, with no touches of completion at all.

The only time I saw Grandmother in a proper hat was when she and Grandfather had a fancy dress party. It wasn't a special occasion. They just liked to have parties and they were not like Mother and Father's parties where everybody just eats dinner and then talks or maybe, once in a while, they have a musicale. G&G's parties always had things to do. Sometimes they put on real plays like *A Midsummer Night's Dream* by William Shakespeare (which I now remember I never described because I got distracted by writing my own plays, but I'll just say that the most surprising thing was that Grandmother painted a forest background right on the wall!) and sometimes they just put on "entertainments." Like "An Arabian Night's Entertainment." Everybody came dressed with embroidered silk shawls draped around them. When Mrs. Hawkins saw them she said, "There are many naked pianos around the neighbourhood this evening."

The men wore baggy trousers in bright colours or their bathrobes and slippers decorated with shiny things. Grandmother made herself a purple velvet turban and stuck feathers in it. Millie and I looked at the drawings in the stories of Aladdin and Ali Baba and we wore shawls tied around our waists and beads around our ankles. Owen would have nothing to do with it except to try to make himself a scimitar but it turned out to be too bendy.

We moved all the rugs into the parlour and put them over low boxes. A young man from somewhere foreign (Russia?) played snakey music on the piano and Mrs. Burns from the village sang songs about harems and love in the desert while gazing at a flower vase. The adults were sillier than the children.

Millie and a young woman called Dora and I performed the dance of the seven veils with the net curtains from the kitchen until Millie stubbed her toe on one of the rug-covered boxes.

Mrs. Hawkins baked some honey cakes and one of the guests brought a sweet called Turkish Delight, which I would like to eat every day of my life. Millie and I had tried to make rosewater by boiling dried rose petals, but that turned into grey, dusty-tasting water so we gave up on helping with the food and there was an ordinary supper later when everyone got tired. Mrs. Hawkins said that being Arabian is all very well but there comes the time when everybody just wants a cup of tea.

I cannot imagine Mr. Niven from Father's bank coming here for a party wearing his bedroom slippers decorated with jewels.

May 28

The Vicar came to our house for dinner today. Here's what happened.

Scene: Our dining room.
Dramatis Personae:
Mr. and Mrs. Wilton, a banker and his wife
The Rev. Hill and Mrs. Hill, a vicar and his wife
Mr. and Mrs. Fraser, people from church
Miss Doughty, head of the altar guild
Dorothy Wilton, *Titanic* survivor

Rev. Hill: So, Mrs. Wilton, what do you think about these suffragette women and the vote and such-like?

(The *Titanic* survivor stops daydreaming and begins to pay attention. This is a subject that was much discussed in Lewisham.)

Mrs. W.: I don't quite see the point. I would obviously vote with . . .
Miss Doughty: Did you see the news of that big march in New York City? Thousands of women, some of them on horseback, parading to show that they wanted the vote. I do wonder. What kind of riff-raff would they encounter on such a march?
Rev. Hill: Estimable women, I'm sure. Estimable but misguided.

Mrs. Hill: Yes, misguided. I feel, as I'm sure you do, Esme, that we make our contribution to the nation by staying home and taking care of our husbands and children. The hand that rocks the cradle rules the world, that's what I say.

Mrs. W.: Yes, we just let the men think they are running things.

(Laughter all round.)

Rev. Hill: You're absolutely right, Esme. Think of the women in the parish, on our altar guild, like excellent Miss Doughty here, and in our ladies' auxiliary, doing such good work. Where would we be without them, I ask you, where would we be?

Mrs. Hill (also known as The Echo): Yes, where would we be?

Mr. Fraser, *smiles at Dorothy:* I have just one thing to say to suffragettes and those who want women and men to be equal: Remember the *Titanic.*

(Nods all round.)

Mr. Wilton: Do you mean because the men let the women and children go first into the lifeboats?

Rev. Hill: Precisely. Male gallantry and courage. Chivalrous self-sacrifice.

(Nods all round, except from Mr. Wilton.)

Mr. Wilton: But, wasn't it also men who said the *Titanic* was unsinkable? Wasn't it men who decided on the number of lifeboats?
(Pause all round. Mrs. Wilton looks startled.)
Rev. Hill, *gives a little laugh, one of those laughs that pretend to be jolly and comical but really the person is sort of peeved:* Well, goodness me, we wouldn't expect women to be marine engineers then, would we? Ha ha. Anyway, enough of this subject. I'm sure Dorothy doesn't want to dwell on the tragedy of that fatal night. Safe home now.
The Echo: Yes, safe home now.
Mrs. Wilton: Would anybody care for a taste more of the trifle?

CURTAIN.

That was a surprise. Father sounded just like Grandfather or Grandmother.

May 29

I've just thought of something. It is completely obvious but I never thought of it before. Father was there. When he was a little boy he sat at that breakfast table and listened to those discussions. Grandmother and Grandfather are his parents, just like Mother and Father are parents to me. Was he in plays? Did Grandmother knit him things in wool dyed with plants? Did he get to play the piano all black keys?

He never talks about when he was a boy except when he rolls his eyes and says things like, "Are they still having Russians in to paint those dreadful pictures on their walls? I'm so happy that your mother runs to wallpaper."

But this evening, at dinner, I knew that he must have had those arguments with Grandfather. *Think for yourself. Take a position and defend it.* Well, he didn't really defend it. It would have made everybody uncomfortable. But he said it. What if women *had* helped plan the *Titanic?*

Something else I wonder. About the Vicar. Does nobody else notice such things? Does nobody notice when somebody is pretending to be one way and really they are being the opposite way? Irene Rudge does this all the time, being extra-courteous to grown-ups and horrid to other girls. I used to want to grow up so much because I thought that would be over. But now it seems it just goes on and on. Perhaps it even gets worse.

May 30

I woke up early. The light was just coming through the lace curtains, making light lace on my coverlet. I noticed that one curtain was not quite closed so I had to get up to pull the other one over to make them match. It was a very pink sunrise. Sunrise or sunset, which is better? Either/Or.

Grandmother and Grandfather played Either/Or all the time. Crumpets or pikelets, horse or bicycle, snowball fight or water fight, pantomime or Punch and Judy, *Alice's Adventures in Wonderland* or *Through the Looking Glass.* When G&G played, they shouted and interrupted each other, slapped the table ("Crumpets, Augusta! Crumpets, hands down!"), always laughing. At first I started saying, "I like both," but that's "waffling" and not allowed. I learned to make a choice and stick with it and argue until . . . until I was blue in the face, but not really. But Mother and Father don't understand Either/Or. They just waffled.

One of the best rounds with Grandfather happened on the riverbank. We had been rowing in the skiff and he was pretending it was the *Titanic*. It was one of the days when he told me facts. So long, so wide, so heavy, so many propellers. The biggest number was three million rivets. "And we'll see it, in just a few weeks. Think of it. You'll tell your grandchildren. It is a marvel of the age. The dock at Southampton is sixteen acres big," he said. "You could fit the whole village on it."

We tied up at our dock, one smithereenth of an acre big. "River or sea?" asked Grandfather.

He had to choose river, of course, because he had one at the bottom of the garden and he had lived in that house since he was a boy. But I had to stand up for Halifax and choose the sea.

Seas have waves.

Rivers go somewhere.

Seas have salty water which holds you up better than fresh water when you're bathing.

You can drink from a river.

Seas have whales.

Grandfather then used one of the Either/Or tricks: win by listing.

Rivers have carp and roach and pike and tench and trout and stickleback . . . and I can't remember the rest of the fish he listed.

He won.

I didn't say that the sea has icebergs. I didn't think about icebergs when I was sitting on a dock on the River Quaggy with my grandfather. If we played again I would choose river.

May 31

Here is a mystery about grown-ups. Why don't they play? Mother and Father never play. Father plays golf and they both play whist but that's not real playing. I mean that they never jump in leaves or build forts or play hide-and-seek. They make the rules, which means that they *could* climb trees and they would be good at it because they are tall enough to reach the lowest branches, but they don't even want to. What is the good of growing up if all you get to do is go to the office or have ladies to tea?

But it is not true that all adults do not play. Grandfather is good at playing.

A PLAY TO PROVE MY POINT

Scene: A sandy bank on the River Quaggy. The roots of the trees make little cubbyholes in the shallow water.

Dramatis Personae:

Grandfather, Grandmother, the Canadian Girl, Owen. (Millie had Girl Guides.)

Props: A picnic in a picnic basket, a message in a bottle, licorice allsorts in a paper sack.

Grandmother: Oh bother, I forgot the salt. Hard-boiled eggs are dreary without salt.

Grandfather: Look! What's that? In the shallows there, green and shiny? Owen, Dorothy, go have a look.

Owen, *holds the CG's hand so that she can lean way out over the roots and grab the mystery,*

which turns out to be a bottle with a cork in it: It looks like there's something in it. A paper or something.
The CG, *gives a whoop:* I've always wanted to find a message in a bottle. Always and always. It is my top most-wanted-thing ever! Open it, quick.

(I really did say this.)

Grandmother: I might forget the salt but I would never forget the corkscrew. Here you go.
(Owen, opens the bottle and pulls out a piece of old, thin, tattered paper. It has brown, spidery writing on it and a map. He hands it to the CG.)
The CG: All it says is, "I leave this treasure, mined from the mountains of the Sierra Madre, to the future. Find it who may. And may it bring you happiness in equal measure to the pain it has visited upon me. Josiah Q. Snedden, Captain, *The Flying Armadillo.*"
Owen: How did a bottle get upstream?
(Everybody ignores Owen.)
Grandmother: Cheese and cress sandwich, anybody?

Grandfather: Augusta! Where is your sense of occasion? Nobody is interested in sandwiches. We are possibly on the brink of an important discovery. Let's have a look at that map. Hmmm, see where the stream bends just beyond that big oak? That looks just like the map.
The CG: What are we waiting for?
Grandmother: I'll stay and guard the picnic from marauders.
(Grandfather, Owen and the CG set off upstream, then across a stile and past a Roman earthwork, all of these things clearly marked on the map. Then past a barn with a weather vane, a giant copper beech tree and a fence post with a white blaze on it.)

(How would they do this on a stage? It would have to be a very big stage.)

The CG: Last clue. A stone wall. There it is. We need to find a green stone with two white rings around it.
Grandfather, *sits against the wall:* This explorer is weary. I'm going to have a sit-down.
(The CG and Owen search the wall. They don't see a green stone with two rings. They start trying to pull out green stones, or stones with rings, or any old stones at all.)

Grandfather: Stop! You'll have the wall falling down. The expedition is a failure, I guess. Come on, at least we have cheese and cress to look forward to.
(Grandfather stands up.)
Owen: There it is! Right where you were sitting. Two rings!
Owen, *pulls out stone and reaches into hole to find paper sack full of licorice allsorts:* Here it is, treasure!
(The treasure seekers return to the picnic site, all the while discussing licorice allsorts):
Blue beady ones are the best because you can suck them and make them last.
No, the layered kind are better because you can eat them layer by layer.
Purists everywhere prefer the plain black licorice bullets.
But only the bullseyes have cocoanut, besides which, they look like a diagram of the Earth with the licorice centre being solid, liquid or gas and the pink part being everything else.
(These pieces of dialogue can be shared among the cast but the CG gets to praise the bullseyes because she really does love those, especially the pink ones.)

Grandfather: Which ones should we save for Augusta and Millie?

CURTAIN.

The treasure did not ruin our appetites at all. We still ate all the sandwiches and hard-boiled eggs, cherry cake and walnut cake, dried plums and ginger beer. Grandmother saved her share of the booty till last and made no offers to share.

But here's what I mean about play. Of course Grandfather wrote the letter and hid the bottle. I figured that out about the time we were climbing over the stile. And Owen knew too, even before. But as long as we pretended to believe in Captain Snedden it was fun. Fun is what grown-ups who say, "Don't get carried away by make-believe," don't understand. If you go along with the make-believe you have fun and you also get licorice bullseyes. Sometimes.

June 1

White Rabbit.

Mrs. Hawkins said that it was good luck to say "White Rabbit" the very first thing when you wake up on the first day of a new month. This morning I remembered and I'm also writing it first thing for extra good luck. My first chance to try it out was April 1st but I forgot because that morning Brownie woke me up by licking my hand, which was over the side of the bed, and I woke with a start and said, "Brownie, stop it," before I remembered the magic words. And on May 1st I forgot about it because I was only thinking about Irene.

It is just silly to think that forgetting to say White Rabbit meant that a ship as big as a city ran into an iceberg as big as a castle. But people say many silly things. They say that naming the *Titanic* the *Titanic* meant that humans were being too proud, and that caused the disaster. They say that when that other ship nearly hit the *Titanic* when we were leaving Southampton — that was an omen. They say that when the stoker stuck his soot-covered head out of the funnel and startled people, it meant something bad. They say that some little dying girl in England woke up the night of the disaster and said, "Why is that ship sinking?" or something like that.

Grandfather said that you cannot know what will happen in the future because it hasn't happened yet. He said that fortune telling and seances and all that are nonsense for gullible people.

Of course he is right. But I am never going to forget to say White Rabbit again. Never.

June 2

There is a special kind of quiet on Sunday afternoons. It feels as though the house has taken off its shoes and put on its slippers and has gone to sleep in an easy chair with the paper across its face.

There was a guest at lunch, Charles's friend Cedric. Cedric is very superior and he ignores me completely. He also has blond eyelashes. I suppose if somebody was extremely congenial I could bear blond eyelashes, but as Cedric is the first person I ever saw with blond eyelashes I do not think they are nice. He and Father talked about cricket. They didn't really talk, they just traded numbers. It was all googlies and silly mid-ons and test averages and centuries. I have noticed this about men when they talk to each other. They just bat numbers and facts back and forth.

And it was just the same in England. Whenever Grandfather was with me and Grandmother he would talk about everything under the sun. When Owen was with me and Millie he was normal too. But when Grandfather and Owen got together it was facts, facts, facts, back and forth. When Father wrote that he had booked me passage on the *Titanic* they started storing up everything they could find out about the ship. The women in the family tried to play pig-in-the-middle and grab the conversation, but it was hard. Tea time would go something like this:

FACTS: **Scene one.**
GF: Three million rivets.
O: Five hundred pounds of grapefruits.
GF: Four funnels, one of them false.
Grandmother: So, what do you think are our chances of having an earthquake today, Dorothy?
The CG: I think we'll be spared this time but I'm quite concerned about rumours of a giant hedgehog in the county.
O: Reciprocating engines . . .
Grandmother: Did I mention to you that the King would be coming to tea tomorrow? I'm wondering if Mrs. H. could be persuaded to make a walnut cake?
Millie: I don't think he would like it. I read in the *Times* that all his teeth have fallen out.
GF: Seventeen-inch–diameter brass bell . . .

And so it went on. They did not let up until Grandmother started to laugh so hard she began to choke, at which point Grandfather stopped spouting facts and gave her a wallop on the back.

June 3

They are still writing about the *Titanic* in the newspaper. Since coming home from England I read the newspaper. Well, parts of the newspaper. Not the bits about the price of rubber.

Before I got on the *Titanic* I didn't think about it very much. I dreaded seasickness. I dreaded Miss Pugh and her annoying habits. I didn't want to come home and leave everyone at Mill House, so I just didn't think ahead. But one morning near the beginning of April, Grandfather was very excited, reading bits from the newspaper about the sea trials of the *Titanic*. This is when they brought the ship from Belfast, where it was made, to Southampton, where I would get aboard. I didn't pay too much attention. It was mostly about speed, which for some funny reason they measure in "knots" on ships. When I think of knots I just think of shoelaces and marionette strings in a muddle. But now when I think of that morning, sitting over breakfast, Grandfather reading to us from behind his paper as we ate our porridge, I remember two things. One is that when they put the ship into reverse it still took half a mile to stop. That's from my school to the Citadel. If it takes that long to stop, I don't understand why ships don't hit icebergs all the time. The other thing I remember is that when they tested the wireless they were able to talk to people in some port three thousand miles away. I wish we had a wireless like that so I could talk to Grandfather and Grandmother right now. I would also like to talk to

Brownie but I don't suppose he would like to wear headphones.

June 4

In school last year we learned how the early explorers of Canada carried pemmican with them, food that lasted a long time and can keep you alive. I feel as though remembering Mill House is like pemmican. I'm saving it, but every so often I can take a small bite. Here is a bite.

One day Grandfather asked me to take a letter to the post office in town. I could go by the road or by the fields. I wanted to go by the fields because there were new lambs, but how would I find my way? So Grandfather drew me a map. I crossed several fields and there were new lambs who came up and were curious, curious, curious and then turned suddenly shy and ran away. I followed the map and collected wool from the fences, and crossed stiles and pretended that I was going to find the entrance to a magic land and I did not notice that I had crossed into a field with a cow, but it wasn't exactly a cow. It was a bull. This was a field that I had to cross diagonally and I was right in the middle when I noticed the bull and he noticed me. He started to walk toward me, very slowly but with determination. I quickly took stock. Was I wearing anything red? Thank goodness I was not because everybody knows that the colour red enrages bulls. So I MADE myself walk calmly and at a steady pace toward the corner of the field where the gate was. But then I saw it, the red stamp on the letter I was carrying, stamp-side out. I quickly stuffed the letter into my jumper and start to run. I could not turn around but I was sure that I heard the bull thundering after me. Cow fields are very lumpy and I tripped and fell but I got up again like a bouncing ball and made it safely to the gate. The bull looked fierce and disappointed.

I was pretty dirty when I got back home (after mailing the letter, which was only a bit crushed), but Grandfather and Grandmother don't mind about things like dirt. When I told my story they both said that I was heroic and brave. But then Grandfather told me that the thing about bulls and red is a myth (not like the myth of Hercules, but just something not true) and that likely the reason the bull came after me was because I started to run. Even though I knew that, I didn't go across that field again. I have not run that fast since I got home.

June 5

This is a bigger bite of pemmican.

Miss Caughey came to tea this afternoon and made me cry. She was not mean. She was exactly the opposite. She brought me a bag of books. She told Mother that I should be reading for pleasure while I am not at school because this will help me in my studies when I return.

As soon as I looked at the books I began to cry because one of them was *The Railway Children,* one of the lost things.

Miss Caughey was very kind and gave me her own hankie to cry into because I had forgotten to put one in my pocket. She told me that E. Nesbit was one of her favourite authors and then I said something that flabbergasted her. Her mouth actually fell open. I told her that I met E. Nesbit — that I went to her house. She wanted to know every little thing about my visit and she let her tea go stone cold in her cup, listening.

Grandmother and Grandfather did a lot of paying visits and they always took me along. On one particular day Grandfather would not tell me where we were going. He was bouncy with a secret and kept saying things like, "Prepare to be amazed."

We went on the train and then in a pony trap and came to a big, three-storey house. It had so much ivy on it that it looked as though it was made of ivy, with just doors and windows cut out. A woman came out to greet us saying, "Here she is! The Canadian." Grandfather introduced her as Mrs. Bland.

She did not match her name at all. She wore an

embroidered dress that had no waist and there was a kind of long coat over that, also embroidered, and she had lots of silver bangles on her arms. Her hair was brown and curly and bits of it were falling down. She was smoking a cigarette. She was stout but she moved as though she was going to start skipping any minute. Whatever the opposite word to *bland* is, that is what she was like.

At first I was shy because she was one of those people who look right at you, but then she took me inside to the drawing-room and showed me something that she had made. It was called "The Magic City" and it was a whole world of miniature buildings laid out on a big table. Temples and pools and cathedrals and towers and arches and other buildings that I don't even know the names of. I did not know what to say until I noticed the dominoes. They were decorating one of the city walls.

As soon as I started to really look I saw chessmen and boxes, books, candlesticks, brass bowls, ashtrays, biscuit tins, ivory figures and a tea-kettle lid. It was magic and funny and it made me long for two things. It made me long to shrink to miniature and explore the city on my own two feet. And it made me long to make a magic city of my own. I told Mrs. Bland, who is the kind of person you tell things to, and she said that of course I must do both things, make my own miniature city and imagine myself small.

By the time we had explored every street and lane, every tall tower and city square, I had forgotten to be shy.

At lunch there were other people but they were all grown-ups and I couldn't sort them out. Grandfather and Mrs. Bland had a big but jolly argument about Shakespeare and bacon.

When I told Miss Caughey about the bacon she burst into laughter and I asked what was funny and she said she would tell me later but first she wanted to hear the rest of my story.

After lunch Mrs. Bland and I went outside, even though it was showery. The garden was like a big room with walls of trees and shrubbery. Brownie raced around and around and we found a ball to play with. There were crocuses and snowdrops and Mrs. Bland told me a story from when she was a little girl. She was all dressed up to go visiting and her mother told her to go outside and stay tidy. But she had older brothers and when they saw her they thought she looked so beautiful, like a flower, that they decided to plant her. So they dug a hole and did just that, planted her in the ground. It was not good for her nice clean dress and of course her mother was furious. I told Mrs. Bland that I had an older brother as well and I knew what it was like to be treated like a toy.

We agreed that it was silly to send children outside and then expect them to stay clean.

Then Mrs. Bland showed me the moat. I didn't know houses had moats, only castles. There was a raft tied up, a raft that seemed to be made of fence pickets. Mrs. Bland told me that she made it and she would have invited me for a ride except that the raft was "unreliable."

The rain let up and we sat by the side of the moat and Mrs. Bland told me how she had lost her temper with some man who had told her that the raft was not properly built. "I have a terrible time with my temper," she said. "Have had, my whole life." Then she asked me if I had that trouble and I said that I didn't and she said that I was very lucky in my disposition because a quick temper was a great trial.

(Of course I was wrong about myself because this was before I slapped Irene Rudge and before Miss Pugh and that night on the *Titanic*, but I'm not going to write about that.)

This was a very odd conversation to be having with a grown-up that you've just met. Mrs. Bland went on to tell me that the solution she had finally come to was that she couldn't help losing her temper, but right after, she would ask herself, "Am I really still angry or am I just enjoying being in a temper?" and mostly she had to admit she was enjoying it, so then she would stop and apologize.

I remember thinking that I didn't know any mothers in Halifax that I could imagine having such a conversation with, or any mother who would build a raft out of fence pickets, or any kind of raft at all. Or a Magic City.

But these were private thoughts so I didn't tell Miss Caughey, but skipped along to the part of the story where Mrs. Bland gave me *The Railway Children* and when she signed it for me was the first time I realized that Mrs. Bland and E. Nesbit were one and the same person. She drew a little clover leaf in the book. Later I saw that the clover leaf was really the letters *EB*, which is for Edith Bland, which is her real, non-book-writing name.

When we got home to Mill House I read that book all in one go, even reading through dinner, which Grandmother doesn't mind. By the time I got to the last chapter I just could not keep my eyes reading so Grandmother read it aloud. We all cried. Even Grandfather, although he pretended not.

I read the book one more time when I was in England. I cried again even though I knew what was going to happen. I don't know why happy endings can make you cry just as much as sad endings.

Mother said that Mrs. Bland sounded rather bohemian and were her books suitable and Miss

Caughey said that her books were excellently written and most suitable and that next time she came she would bring one called *Five Children and It.*

I've already started *The Railway Children* again. I'm at the end of chapter one, which is when they think that the noises in their new house are rats.

I have the whole of "The Jumblies" by heart now and when I recited it to Miss Caughey she applauded and said I was a champion elocutionist. On her way out the door she asked if I was writing about my time on the *Titanic* and I said that I didn't know how to start. She said I should start small and she gave me one question to answer.

June 6

I forgot to explain about Shakespeare and the bacon. It is Bacon, not bacon. Miss Caughey says that some people think that Shakespeare didn't write his own plays but left it to somebody named Mr. Bacon. Imagine being named Mr. Bacon. It is like being named Mr. Pork Chop or Miss Mutton.

I am thinking about Miss Caughey's question.

June 7

Letters from Mill House today. Millie did well in her school examinations. Owen did not mention his. They are going to stay with some cousins in the Lake

District for the summer holiday. I am jealous, not of Owen and Millie, but of the cousins, who will have them to play with. Mrs. Hawkins says that the perennial border that I helped weed ("You are a champion weeder, unlike some loll-about children I could name.") is looking glorious. Grandfather stepped in a rabbit hole and turned his ankle. Grandmother went up to London to be on a committee.

June 8

All right. Miss Caughey's question was: How was your cabin on board the *Titanic* different from your room at home?

The first thing that was different is that at home everything is a mixture of very old (like my bed, which belonged to Granny Mackenzie), a bit old (like my bedside rug that Mother hooked when she was just a girl), and some new (like my new clothes), but on the ship *everything* was new. The carpet was new, the beds were new, the walls were new, the sheets were new, the wash basin was new. It smelled new, like paint and polish. It was funny to think that I was the first person to ever sleep in the bed, just as I was the first person in the dining room to eat from the china and the first person on deck to run my hands along a bit of railing. I can't imagine another place you could be where every single part was new, except maybe in the world on the day after Creation, but then Adam and Eve didn't have beds and wash basins to appreciate. Or even clothes until they sewed those fig leaves together to make aprons.

Second thing is that the walls in my room here have wallpaper and the walls in the cabin were shiny white. Wallpaper is more interesting, especially if you are home in bed sick. I have travelled miles in my mind around the ivy on my wallpaper.

The third different thing was the washstand. The basin was in a dark wood cabinet and it folded up toward the wall. When you washed you pulled it down toward you and pressed a button and water came from somewhere behind the mirror. When you were done, the water drained away to a hidden bucket.

Of course the stewardess brought hot water in a jug when we needed it, but we could pull down the basin whenever we liked. I liked the gush of water when I filled the basin and the gurgle when it drained out, but Miss Pugh told me I was washing my hands far too often.

The fourth thing is that the bed had a curtain. I had the upper berth and I could pull the curtain across and be in a small room of my own, with my own electric reading light. Mother told me that when I was small I always liked to hide in small spaces, like under the bed, or under the table, or under bushes in the garden.

I would like a bed with a curtain all the time. I like to be able to reach out and touch all the edges of the darkness at night. I don't like it when the darkness stretches out and you can't see where it ends.

June 9

Last night I had the melting dream. It is always the same. At least the melting is always the same. I am in a crowd of people. I reach up and take somebody's hand and it is cold and then I look into the faces and they are all staring and then the faces begin to melt. When I write this down it does not seem so frightening, but when I am in the dream it is so terrifying that all I can do is haul myself out of it and wake up.

In the middle of the night the Jumblies lines I recite to myself are, "O Timballoo! How happy we are when we live in a sieve and a crockery jar." I say them over and over again until I fall back asleep.

This morning, thinking about the trip to London with Grandfather, thinking about what to say in this journal, I have remembered something which might explain where the dream came from.

To get to the dock in Southampton we had to take a special train from Waterloo Station in London at 7:30 in the morning, so Grandfather and I went up to London the day before. Grandmother had to stay home for a meeting about poverty. She said that Grandfather should take me to the British Museum, which would be very educational.

When we arrived in London, however, Grandfather asked if I would mind very much if we didn't go to the British Museum but to another museum called Madame Tussaud's. He said that he had always wanted to visit it but that Grandmother never wanted to see it because she said it was vulgar. Of course I didn't know anything about either museum so I said fine. It turned out that Madame Tussaud's was a wax museum, which is a building where they have statues, made out of wax, of famous people. It was amazing. Everything about the statues looked alive — the colours, their clothes, their hair. You just think that at any moment they are going to start walking and talking. We saw Queen Elizabeth and Benjamin Franklin and Marie Antoinette. There was a room called the Chamber of Horrors and Grandfather thought he should not take me in, but I wanted to go. It was all about murders and criminals. It was that kind of scary that you let yourself be scared, like listening to a ghost story. Some grown-ups might say that Grandfather should not have taken me to the Chamber of Horrors, but the dream is not about the guillotine or Jack the Ripper. It is just about faces, staring eyes.

June 10

It is very hard to make my bed properly since Mother put on the summer blanket, which does not have any stripes. I have to wake up earlier to have time to do it before breakfast.

Today we are going to Larsens' to shop for new shoes for me. My feet are already bigger than Mother's. I wonder when they will stop growing. I wonder when I will stop growing taller. Is there a moment when you know that you are your proper size for life? Charles had a friend who grew two inches taller after he was twenty years old! He had to replace all his suits.

All right. London.

When Grandfather and I got to Waterloo Station there was a great hubbub of people and luggage. We had arranged to meet Miss Pugh at the ticket office and she was there, waiting for us.

June 11

I had to stop writing yesterday because of Miss Pugh. I have already torn out two pages, but this time I am going to write it and leave it.

I did not like Miss Pugh. That's the plain truth.

Everyone said how convenient it was that Miss Pugh was going to England to visit her aged father and could accompany me on my journey. Nobody cared that I knew her only as somebody who worked in Father's bank. "Our estimable Miss Pugh," Father called her.

She might have been estimable but I did not like her. She tried to act as though she were my mother or my teacher but all she was supposed to do was accompany me to England and back again. She was fussy and finicky and she would not admit when she was wrong. She treated Beryl, our stewardess on the ship, like she (Miss Pugh) was Lady Astor or some other rich and famous person and Beryl was a servant, but all the time Beryl knew much more than she did, about the ship and many other things, as well as being much NICER. Miss Pugh made a funny noise with her teeth and she smelled like liniment.

For the whole voyage Miss Pugh seemed to want to correct me. She corrected the way I tied my hair ribbons because they were not tidy enough. She corrected the words I used. When I said that the curly backs of the chairs in the dining room were "baroque" she said I was being overly fanciful. She corrected my table manners. I know you are not supposed to talk with your mouth full, but adults ignore this rule all the time. If you obey this rule and chew and swallow before you say anything, then the conversation has moved on and you never get a chance to say anything at all. If I questioned her she said I was "argumentative."

The worst thing was that she was so boring. She never wanted to talk about anything interesting. For example, is grass green at night in the dark? Or is it green only when light is on it, making it green? And does that mean that grass might not be green at all? Grandfather would have loved to talk about this. But when I asked Miss Pugh she just said, "That's a big question for a little girl."

What can you say to that, except be quiet and grind your teeth and not be argumentative.

I did not like Miss Pugh.

But I did not want her to die.

It was my fault.

I'm the only person alive who knows what happened.

I know that I have to finish the story because finishing it is like straightening the bed or ironing the napkins perfectly. I can't not do it. I know that I can always tear out these pages or I can throw away the whole thing so that nobody will ever find it.

But I don't have the heart to write any more plays. Tomorrow I will begin again about the *Titanic*.

June 12

I am in the garden. Asquith is hiding in the rhubarb to ambush Borden. Borden is a very patient dog.

Waterloo Station. I had resolved to be pleasant and polite with Miss Pugh. I had taken Mrs. Bland's words to heart and I promised myself that I would not lose my temper. As Grandfather and I walked toward the ticket office I floated up into the highest part of the station, with the pigeons, looked down and said, "Who is that very well-behaved child?" My good intentions lasted less than ten minutes.

They lasted while Grandfather said goodbye and while I cried a wee bit and while he made a silly joke about bullfighting in Nova Scotia. They lasted until Grandfather produced a bag of sweets from his pocket "for the train" and Miss Pugh sniffed and said they were "unsuitable for 7:30 a.m."

In all my time in Lewisham I never heard anybody say "unsuitable." I heard "wicked" and "vulgar" and "outrageous." I heard "horror" and "misery" (mostly to do with housework). I even heard "damned" (even though I don't think I was supposed to; I was under the table and they had forgotten me). But I never heard "unsuitable." "Unsuitable" is a word used by people who sniff.

So Grandfather left and I was sad — which can sometimes be almost a good feeling — and sullen, which never is. The pigeons looked down and said to each other, "Who is that willful and unpleasant child?"

No bad feeling could last on the train. Miss Pugh read her book and sniffed and I ate my sweets and looked out the window and memorized the stations. Surbiton, Woking, Basingstoke, Winchester, East-leigh. Barley sugar, humbugs, pear drops, jelly babies, licorice allsorts (with extra pink bullseyes).

Mother has just come to tell me that Aunt Hazel has dropped by and I'm to come inside and be sociable.

June 12 (later)

I'm interrupting my story for one piece of big news: Aunt Hazel and Uncle Leslie have ordered a motor car! It is called the Tudhope Torpedo.

All right, back to the ship.

When Miss Pugh and I got to Southampton we went right on board the ship, up the gangway, like crossing the drawbridge to a castle. The second-class entrance was on C deck at the aft end. (That's ship's talk for *back.*) So many people got on at the same time that we were like a river. I noticed some men with musical instruments in cases and I heard a woman say that they were the ship's orchestra.

As soon as we were aboard, Miss Pugh started to fuss. That is the difference between us. I thought almost everything was fun and she thought almost everything was fuss. Luggage, for example. The stewards have quite a time getting the luggage to the cabins. It is all in a great heap and they have to find everybody's things. Later on, when I got to know Beryl, she told me that sometimes the luggage tags fall off and then it is all chaos. People wander about, asking questions, getting lost, talking to their friends as though they are on a crowded street in London. Through all this the stewards have to move the luggage without knocking anybody on the head or dropping a steamer trunk on their foot. It is like watching a farmer and his dogs round up cows. Who would not enjoy watching it? The answer is Miss Pugh. She just fussed and worried about our own luggage. Where was it? When would we get it? What if it were lost?

All the time she was totally ignoring the really important things — like should we take the red-carpeted stairs or the electric lift and did you see that woman who had a squeaky little dog that looks *exactly* like her?

Finding our cabin was confusing. We were on D deck. Miss Pugh took the stairs and I took the lift. Miss Pugh thought we might lose each other. I rather hoped we would. The numbers on the rooms didn't really make sense so everybody was asking questions of the stewards. "I can find D-70 but where is D-71?" It was like a maze. Some of the adults were quite cross but every child I saw was enjoying the muddle.

When we got to our cabin there was no luggage there, which sent Miss Pugh into a tizzy. But in a few minutes a steward named Jack brought everything. Then a stewardess appeared to help us sort ourselves out. She was a young woman and very pretty. She introduced herself as Miss Beryl Cope but said that we should call her Beryl. Of course I had no way of knowing what an important person she would be.

The cabin was like a playhouse, everything fitted and tidy. Miss Pugh said that we should unpack and settle in, but I could hear lots of commotion outside the cabin and I was longing to see what was what.

In the middle of one of Miss Pugh's fusses, Beryl said that it would all be much easier if I were not underfoot. At first I was cross and thought Beryl was one of those people who think all children are a bother and who say things like "underfoot" as though we are pets. My temper started to feel bigger than the cabin, but then Beryl said that the best way to get one's bearings was to go around the ship and explore because, after all, it was impossible to get lost. Miss Pugh's head was in a valise at this moment and Beryl winked at me. So Miss Pugh said, "Off you go then," and I knew Beryl was a friend.

"Go and look at first class," said Beryl. "Last chance."

The way things work on a ship is that everything goes by class — first, second and third. Each class has its own dining room and lounge and cabins. And usually everybody stays in their class, but that first morning people were here, there and everywhere, bustling about. Nobody paid any attention to me. If you want to be invisible, find a bustling crowd.

As I stuck my head in the fancy rooms I realized what all the *Titanic* fuss was about. It was the fanciest place anyone could think of, like the wonderful house that Aladdin orders up or the ivory palace in the Bible. Who would think to bring whole palm trees inside and plant them in pots or to have ivy growing up the walls? Who would think to paint a room light green and pink? (I would like my bedroom to be light green and pink but I don't think Mother would let me have it.)

Going with the tide of people, I ended up at the grand staircase. In the illustrated papers they always show a photograph of this staircase, but what the pictures don't show is how shiny everything was. The light came in from a huge glass dome and sparkled off the polished wood and the gold decorations on the railings and the angel holding a torch. The pictures also miss out the smells — furniture polish and flowers.

Next to the stairway was the elevator, so I took it

down to E deck. Even it was fancy, with wood panelling and clever doors. The lift operator was handsome and shy and he looked as young as a schoolboy. Later on I found out his name was Fred. From E deck I found stairs (well, I called them stairs then) to go up and down. It was all a great hubbub and nobody paid any heed to me. I wasn't looking for anything in particular so everything I found was a discovery.

I think it must have been like this for the great explorers. Of course they were looking for things, like Columbus looking for India (Was he looking for India? I might have got that muddled) or like Captain Scott looking for the South Pole, but everything they found was new, so everything was a discovery. I don't think there is much left to discover now that Mr. Amundsen has found the South Pole.

I got a look into the bathing pool. It didn't have any water in it yet. I think it must have been odd to swim in water while sailing on water. Of course I didn't get a chance to find out because it was only for first-class passengers.

But I almost got to use the gymnasium! It was up on the boat deck and when I poked my head in, there were people using all the different machines. The exercise instructor, dressed all in white and looking very strong and healthy, was going from one to the other. There was a rowing machine and two stationary bicycles and, funniest of all, an electric camel and an electric horse. They didn't really look like a camel or a horse but like complicated machines with seats, and they just seemed to jiggle the riders up and down and make them laugh. Then two photographers came in and the instructor asked who wanted to have their picture taken.

Everybody laughed and I thought, "Why not me?" But just as I was getting my courage together, a man and a woman who were on the bicycles volunteered. After the photographers had gone, the instructor said that they were from a London illustrated paper and that the photographs would likely be published.

Then I did wish I had volunteered. Imagine if Grandfather had opened up his paper and seen me on an electric camel!

My writing hand is tired. So many words and the ship has not even left. One morning on the *Titanic* was like a week anywhere else.

June 13

I wish I had a typewriter. They have one at Father's bank. Once you master it you can make the words come out quickly, and best of all, they are very neat.

After I didn't have my photograph taken, the tide

of people moved toward the decks as all the visitors went ashore and the time came for the ship to pull away from the dock. Everyone was laughing and talking to strangers, the way people do when they're at a fair or starting on a holiday. There was a man standing near me who was one of those people who like to tell you things. Perhaps he was a schoolteacher or a minister or some other Mr. Chatty. At any rate he was giving lessons to anyone who would listen.

The tugboats seemed so small, dancing around the huge ship, drifting black smoke around them.

Mr. Chatty named all the tugs. *Hercules* and *Neptune* and *Ajax* and other big hero names, which nobody ever names their sons nowadays. Except now I remember there was one called *Albert*. I don't know how he got in there.

You could smell burning coal in the air. The steam whistle blew three great blasts and everyone cheered. The people on the ship threw flowers and the people on shore waved their scarves and handkerchiefs.

Mr. Chatty kept on sharing information.

"There go the mooring lines. We're off!"

"They'll tow us to the turning circle."

"Hear that jangle? That means 'Ahead slow.'"

"Feel that? That's the propellers starting."

We started to go forward. At first you could hardly

feel it and then we started to move and then go faster. Then Mr. Chatty said, "Look there. Look at the *New York.* Something's amiss there."

He did not mean the city. There was another big ship there and the back of it was swerving around toward us. Then there was a shudder and the *Titanic* stopped going forward, paused and began to go backward. We moved right past the back (I mean stern) of the other ship. Then there was a delay in which Mr. Chatty kept on, but I had had my fill of lessons and wanted to do more exploring.

I have moved out to the garden because Mother says it is too nice a day to be inside. Borden has gone into hiding and Asquith is pretending to hunt birds. Back to the *Titanic.*

I did not hear anyone else mention the *New York* and how they nearly hit us. It wasn't until later, after the disaster, that people started to say that it was an omen.

People say something was an omen when they want to show off, when they want to say that they knew something was going to happen. I remember Grandfather saying that fortune tellers are nonsense because the reason the future is the future is because it hasn't happened yet.

Irene always says that things are omens. Once a

bird pooped on her in the schoolyard and she said that she knew it was going to happen, that when she woke up she had a "feeling." I asked her if she had told her feeling to the bird so he could aim at her head and she just tossed her head and did not reply. Of course I did not really expect her to reply because the question was rhetorical. Mother says that I should not ask rhetorical questions because they make me look forward and saucy. However I like them.

Our first meal was lunch. On the way to England I didn't eat a single meal in the dining room so I did not know that you ate at the same table with the same people every time. They were like your family for the crossing.

The six people at our table were an English lady who was going to Oregon to marry a man who had a fruit farm, a clergyman and his wife, and a Scottish family who were moving to Seattle to start a hotel. The Scottish girl and her mother had very stylish clothes and I thought the girl, who was fifteen, might be a friend, but she and her mother turned out to be rather superior. They made sure we knew that they were more used to travelling in first class. They did say that second class on the *Titanic* was much like first class on other ships, but they said it as though they were being kind to us by sitting at our table.

At first I was afraid of the clergyman because he had fearsome eyebrows that stuck out of his forehead like a badger. (Do I mean a badger? Do badgers have eyebrows? Badger-coloured, anyway.) But then he started to tell a story about a man who ran over somebody's chicken and as he was telling the story he was fiddling with his napkin. Then, at the final line of the story, he gave the napkin a sharp twist and pull and it turned into a shape just like a plucked chicken ready for the oven. Everybody laughed, except his wife, who groaned and said, "Oh, Cyril," but in a kind way, and Miss Pugh, who looked as though she had a pain. The next day he showed me how to do it.

The chicken trick was also good because it made me notice a girl of about my age who was sitting at the next table. She had observed the chicken and she had a great loud laugh. Her mother shushed her and I knew right away that I liked her and that her mother was always shushing her and that we must try to get together.

Miss Pugh only wanted to talk about the famous people in first class and thank goodness the Scottish mother and daughter were also interested in this tedious topic so that they could go on and on about the Astors and the Guggenheims and Lady this and the Countess of that. When they got to a long discussion of how a woman in first class was travelling with fourteen trunks, the clergyman's eyebrows started to twitch.

After lunch Miss Pugh wanted to have a nap so Beryl said she would show me the promenade and library on C deck. Then she had to go and answer some bells. Beryl was always answering bells. On the way up the stairs she told me the proper names for parts of the ship. Staircases between decks are called "companionways" and the corridor outside our rooms is an "alleyway." The walls of the alleyways are called "bulkheads." Beryl said that if I want to be a real sailor I should call them by their proper names. After that, whenever I heard Miss Pugh say "the wall of the *corridor*" I felt quite superior.

When I got to the library I was happy to see that the loud-laughing girl from lunch was there and we started to talk right away. I found out that her name was Marjorie and that she was eleven. She was travelling with her parents and they were going to join her grandfather in California.

She said right away that we must plan to sneak into somewhere that we are not allowed to go.

I did not want to get into trouble, but something about Marjorie meant you could not say no to her ideas. "Like first class?" I asked. Miss Pugh had made much of the fact that we were not allowed to go into first class and, oh, if she could only see it.

But Marjorie said that first class was all about hats and china and staircases and it would be better to try to sneak into the engine room or the kennels. Somehow she knew that there were kennels on the boat deck for all the bigger dogs. Then I asked her if she had seen the woman who looked just like her dog and she had and she laughed her loud laugh and the people quietly reading or writing postcards looked at us in a shushing sort of way and I knew that Marjorie was going to be the kind of friend who might get me into trouble but that it would be worth it.

Around sunset we arrived in Cherbourg in France to board more passengers. They came out to the ship in smaller boats with all their luggage. Marjorie and I invented a game of picking out one embarking passenger group and waving furiously to them as though we knew them. It was comical to see them looking friendly and confused.

In between all the things that happened that first day I thought about seasickness. I kept waiting for that dreadful feeling that starts somewhere behind your nose and ends up in every part of you, including the tips of your toes. But it never happened. Miss Pugh had told Beryl I was prone to seasickness and Beryl said I was to spend as much time on deck as possible and look at the far horizon, but that a smooth crossing was predicted and anyway, I looked like a girl who had her sea legs.

The first night on board I could not go to sleep. I had so many stories going on in my head, stories of Mill House and stories of home. But mostly it was the delicious feeling of being in between. I didn't want to sleep and miss anything. I didn't want to sleep and miss the pleasure of my secret bed-cave.

I could still hear Miss Pugh sniffing and snoring, but at least I could not see her teeth.

On the way to England I just hated Miss Pugh's false teeth. She kept them in a glass of water on the washstand. I tried not to look at them but my glance just kept going there, the way you can't help picking a scab on your knee. And even when the light was out I sensed them there, floating in the water, grinning. On the *Titanic* I made sure that I did not peek out of my curtain until I heard Miss Pugh up and about, with her teeth safely in her mouth.

June 14

Mother came in this morning as I was writing in this journal. She asked me how I was getting on. I said it was fine. Then she told me I had very nice penmanship.

Something was up. Mother does not believe in praising children, for penmanship or anything else. She seemed awkward and if she had been a girl I would have said she was shy. She sat on the edge of the bed.

Then she said, "We must have read your postcard a hundred times when we were waiting for news of you."

Truth was, I had forgotten the postcard. The first evening on board I wrote two postcards, to Mother and Father and to Grandmother and Grandfather, because Miss Pugh told me that they would take off the mail the next morning in Ireland and it would be our last chance to send it.

Mother then went on to tell me what it was like when they were waiting for word of the ship. They woke up on Monday morning to the news. "We did not know what to believe," she told me. The first edition of the newspaper said that the *Titanic* was in danger. The second edition said that everyone was safe. She told me that she and Father went down to the White Star offices to wait for information and they were told that the survivors would be taken to Halifax. At noon they heard that the *Titanic* was going to be towed. Then Mother said, "All the time we had just one question: Is Dorothy safe?" As the day went on the news got worse and worse and finally, late on Monday night, a rumour started that the *Titanic* had sunk, and then the rumour was confirmed.

"We did not sleep all night," said Mother. "The neighbours came over. We kept making pots of tea and not drinking them. Time stopped. And Asquith went out after dinner and did not come home. I got it into my head that if Asquith was safe, so were you, so I made Father walk around the streets with a piece of fish on a string, calling his name."

I was surprised. Mother often complains about Asquith's fur and the way he scratches the furniture and the way he always wants to be in when he's out and out when he's in.

So I just said it. "You don't even like Asquith."

Mother laughed a small laugh and motioned me to come and sit beside her on the bed. "It was superstition. The worry of you was so big that I needed a smaller worry, a cat-sized worry. Father could not find Asquith anywhere. He was gone all night."

Then she told me that on Tuesday morning they finally got news that I was safe on board the *Carpathia,* which was on its way to New York.

"As soon as we got the news, Asquith turned up again."

I asked Mother why she hadn't told me all this before and she said that she didn't want to remind me of things that I would rather forget.

Then she remembered that she was a mother and commented on my inky fingers and hoped I wasn't going to get ink on my sheets and, goodness me, look at the time.

So it was just like England. The newspaper printed stories that weren't true. Did the people who wrote those stories get in trouble later?

Later

Back to the ship.

One of the pleasantest things about life on board the ship was that Miss Pugh left me alone to wander. On the morning of the second day she found a missionary lady from India to talk to and they spent most of the day together.

It was very easy to get lost with all the alleyways and decks, but I have a very good Bump of Locality and it didn't worry me because how lost can you get? That morning I found an enclosed area on C deck where there were a couple of toddlers playing with a top and some blocks. They were boys, as pretty as can be, with shiny brown curls. Even the older one couldn't manage the top, so I sat down with them. Their father sat close and was very attentive but he didn't actually play with the boys. The bigger boy was very kind to the smaller one.

Usually children like me. I'm always happy to mind little ones. But these boys wouldn't seem to talk when I asked them questions. Then their father said something to them and I realized it was French. I was so excited. Here was a chance to try out my French.

And, luckily, I knew just the sort of questions you can ask little children, like "What is your name?" and "How old are you?" I even remembered to use "*toi*" because they were children. At first they giggled and hid their eyes behind their hands, so I decided to sing the one French song I know, which was "*A la Claire Fontaine.*" I just sang it very quietly, to myself, and soon they were cuddling up to me.

From then on we were great friends and I found out that their names were Lolo and Momon and that they were three and one. Mostly our conversation was things like I would point to my hand and say "*Main?*" and Lolo would nod. We did this with all the body parts I knew. Then I started to do it wrong, pointing to my nose and saying, "*Pied?*" Lolo roared "*Non*" and then I said "*Oui*" and he said "*Non*" and then he started to laugh so hard he got the hiccups. One of the nice things about being with small children is that they think you are very funny.

Their father smiled a bit but he didn't say a word to me.

Later that morning I took Marjorie back to that part of the deck. She hadn't discovered it yet. By this time there were a number of other small children and when I started to talk to Momon and Lolo (well, if you can call it talking when all you do is point to your ear and say "*Genou*") another French child came over, a little girl called Simone with a big bow in her hair. She found me funny as well. Her mother and baby sister were there, but again, the father of the boys didn't talk to anyone. Maybe because there were no other fathers there. I think Marjorie was impressed by my skill at French!

But she wasn't so fond of little children so we went off to do more exploring.

June 15

That second day Marjorie and I decided to skip lunch so that we could watch everyone coming onboard at Queenstown in Ireland.

More people, more baggage, more confusion.

Mr. Chatty came by and told us that some Irish women had come out from the port to set up a market on the aft deck, so we made our way there. It was linens and lace and things. Many of the rich first-class people were very busy buying so I guess those Irish women were happy when they got in the little boats going back to the dock.

When we departed from Ireland a man played the bagpipes on the aft deck. Bagpipes make a good kind of sad sound, like playing on the black keys.

Then we went to search for the dog kennels, which we finally found behind the fourth funnel. We spent the afternoon visiting the dogs. (And also some chickens who were travelling as somebody's pets. These were not as pleasant as the dogs.) A nice steward named Joe let us help walk them (dogs, not chickens!) and then he brought us some sandwiches because we were hungry, what with skipping lunch. Turned out that Joe was a pal of Beryl's. They had been on several ships together.

There is nothing quite as nice as a picnic in a dog kennel.

June 16

By Friday I felt as though I had been on the ship forever. Marjorie and I had explored all the places we were allowed and some that we weren't. We had sorted out the room numbers. Joe had given us a glimpse into the galley. We knew all the different ways to get from here to there. We knew that the ship's bugler was called Mr. Fletcher and that one of the passengers made the stewardess deliver special meals to her cabin for her Pekinese dog!

Mr. Chatty kept popping up everywhere, always with several facts. "Do you know how many sardines they loaded on? Twenty-five cases, that's how many. What about cigars? What do you think, eh? How many? Eight thousand. Fancy that!"

Marjorie understood completely how amusing it is to make up stories about strangers. For example, one of the couples we kept an eye on was a beautiful young French woman and her older husband. She spent a lot of time in the library playing Patience. He would look over her shoulder and whisper things in her ear and then they would giggle and he would sometimes kiss her on the neck. Marjorie said what if they were not married at all but just "living in sin." I don't know what living in sin means but I didn't let on to Marjorie. It sounded wicked but interesting, a bit like D'Artagnan.

I'm sure Miss Pugh would have thought it most unsuitable for Marjorie and me to talk about such things, whatever such things are.

That was also the day that we got a glimpse of Captain Smith. Beryl told us that he did an inspection each day and that we might expect to see him in the second-class library sometime after ten-thirty. So we waited in the library playing tic tac toe on the stationery and trying not to giggle and, sure enough, he appeared. He was with other men in uniform and he looked splendid, with gold buttons and braid, white gloves, medals and a very tidy white beard and moustache. He seemed like a bishop, or maybe a king. I guess he was like a king, the king of the ship. Actually he looked a bit like King George on the stamps. At least the beard was the same.

We followed the captain out onto the covered

promenade deck. We tried to look as though we just happened to be going that way. The little children were there, as usual. He patted the head of the older of the little French sisters. I understand why because she had thick hair that looked bouncy. I had wanted to pat it myself. Then he said something to the other important men and they all gave little laughs. I guess if you are really important and you make a little joke, everybody laughs. I would like that. When I make a joke at dinner at home nobody pays much attention. Except at Grandfather and Grandmother's house, where all the grown-ups paid attention to anything I said.

Later I told Beryl that I would like to marry a sea captain because Captain Smith looked so clean and important. She laughed and said that that was a good plan because sea captains had lots of money and they were mostly away at sea and wouldn't be much of a bother. Miss Pugh, who overheard this conversation, looked disapproving.

There was also no escaping Mr. Chatty. He gave a lecture to some of the people in the library on how fast the ship was travelling. He said that there was a rumour that the captain was going to try to go very fast so as to make the fastest transatlantic crossing ever, and that on Sunday they were going to fire up all the boilers and make a dash for it. But he,

Mr. Chatty, wanted to set everybody straight: *Titanic* was much slower than *Lusitania* and *Mauretania* and had no hope of setting a speed record.

June 17

What was the best thing about life aboard the *Titanic*? Lovely food? Fancy rooms? Being waited on? Glimpses of famous people?

No. The best thing about the *Titanic* was Marjorie. She was an instant friend. It was as though we took weeks or months of becoming friends and fitted it into four days. She was fun and she had wonderful ideas and she understood completely about Miss Pugh.

Miss Pugh did not approve of Marjorie. She thought she was forward and an unsuitable friend for me. "She has a defiant look on her face, that girl, and her family, well . . . " I knew Miss Pugh wanted me to ask, "What *about* her family?" but I didn't, because I did not want to give Miss Pugh the satisfaction of telling me, whatever it was. She was standoffish with Marjorie's parents, which is the kind of bad behaviour that adults get away with.

I *was* badly behaved. I admit it. I deliberately bothered Miss Pugh. I pulled faces at Marjorie in the dining room to make us both giggle. I sighed loudly when Miss Pugh corrected me. I stared at her mouth when she talked to me instead of looking at her eyes.

Every night I drummed my knuckles softly against the edge of my bed to see how loud I could get before she scolded me. I didn't care a button. I didn't care a fig.

Being on the ship, in that between world, I felt that I could get away with being disobedient, and I enjoyed it.

I might have to tear this page out later.

June 18

On Sunday Marjorie and I got to see Captain Smith again because he took a morning service in the first-class dining room.

Marjorie found out about the service and asked if she could come with me and Miss Pugh. I asked why she wasn't going with her parents and she said it was a big secret but she would tell me later. "Just tell Miss Pugh that my parents are not able to attend." So that's what I told Miss Pugh. She wasn't paying much attention because she and her friend were discussing which famous people they might see.

I was surprised that a captain of a ship could take a church service. I didn't know that a captain is like a vicar. There were lots of people there. Perhaps they all go to church every Sunday at home or perhaps the second-class passengers just wanted a good look at the first-class dining room. Mr. Chatty was there, sitting near us. "Largest room afloat in the history of the world," he declared.

It was certainly bigger than church at home, and a lot more comfortable, with big soft armchairs for everyone to sit in. And with a better view, through big windows out to sea.

The view was distracting and so were the hats, which were much more splendid than the hats at St. Mark's Church in Halifax. The hat ahead of me was as big as a soup tureen. It had wide green velvet ribbon around the edge and silk flowers and leaves sewn onto the ribbon. I spent some time memorizing it and wondering whether I would like to be a milliner. I would like to have all that velvet and silk to play with, but my sewing is not very neat.

After the service Marjorie and I managed to stay around the dining room and watch the people leaving before we had to return to the second-class dining room for lunch. We played "pick the best beard" but we both agreed that Captain Smith's was the nicest. Then Marjorie confessed her secret, in a whisper. (Marjorie likes to whisper.) The secret was that she is R.C., which means Roman Catholic, and that she and her parents had already been to mass earlier that morning, but she wanted to come with me to see the rest of the rich people. I was a bit shocked. I don't know any R.C. people here at home and I wondered if it was right for an R.C. person to go to a Protestant service. But she was Marjorie, just as before, and she wanted to go and see if any dogs were being walked so we did that.

Later I figured out that that was why Miss Pugh did not approve of Marjorie and her parents, because they were R.C.

June 21

I have not written in a few days because I don't want to do this. But I will do it.

Here is what I have not told anyone. I have not told anyone about the pureed turnips. The pureed turnips were the last straw.

Dinner on that last night was lovely. I had turkey with cranberry sauce. It came with green peas and pureed turnip. I like peas. In fact, I like almost all things to eat. But I do not like turnip. Turnip smells like a lavatory. This is one of those true things that nobody says. I did not say this to Miss Pugh. I said, in a very ladylike way, that I did not care for turnip. Then she said that turnip was very good for me and that unless I ate it I could not have dessert. She was treating me like a five-year-old! Nobody has ever made me eat turnip. Mother says that the dinner table is not to be a war zone and that we are allowed to say "no, thank you" to anything. (Except cod liver oil, but that is just a trial to be borne.) The dessert was cocoanut sandwich, which sounded mysteriously good, and American ice cream, which was less mysterious but just as wonderful sounding.

I did not eat my turnip and when the waiter came to take the plates and ask for our dessert orders I piped up quick-like and ordered ice cream. Miss Pugh looked furious but of course she did not want to make a fuss and call attention to us.

Later, in our cabin, she gave me a thorough dressing down. She told me that I was a wicked, spoiled, willful girl and that she expected that I would come to a bad end. I waited her out and said nothing. I blotted out her words by saying, inside my head, over and over, "Soon I will be home."

Then she said that she was going to go to the hymn sing and she expected me to be asleep by the time she returned. I said that I didn't want to go to some dull hymn sing anyway and then I put on my nightgown in an angry sort of way. I didn't brush my teeth.

After she left I was furious. I just needed to do something dreadful. So I started throwing things around, clothes and shoes and bedclothes and books. I pulled her bed apart. I even emptied out the little bag she kept her curlers in. It felt good. Everything I had kept inside when she was saying how bad I was just came bubbling out.

Then I climbed up to my berth, pulled the curtain across, turned out the light and went right to sleep. I did not hear her come back.

The next thing I knew

I can't do it.

June 22

I would like to keep writing about the turnips. Turnips are from before the night of the disaster. The night of the disaster is a line, like the line in history between B.C. and A.D. or the fence around the edge of the graveyard. Everything before I went to sleep that night is before and everything from when I woke up is after. So I am going to write about everything that happened and I'm not going to stop until I am done, for if I stop I might not start again.

I woke up on Sunday night to a crunching sound. It wasn't a crash like when I crashed into a tree at the bottom of the toboggan run last winter. It was more like a shiver. I lay very still because I did not want to talk to Miss Pugh. I was still worried about the clothes strewn about. I listened and listened but I did not hear her moving, only that little strangled snore that she made. I needed to scratch my nose but I didn't want to move. I think I must have slipped into sleep again. In that sleep I thought I heard some kerfuffle and a man's voice but I didn't really wake up.

The next thing I remember was Beryl throwing aside the curtain on my berth and saying, "What is going on here? You need to be on the boat deck," in a very stern way. Miss Pugh was saying dithery things about it being a drill and all she seemed to do was try to take the curlers out of her hair. Then Beryl lifted me down and pushed shoes on my feet, put my coat over my nightgown and my lifebelt over that, wrapped a blanket around me and pulled me out the door, all before I had really woken up. As Beryl left the cabin she said to Miss Pugh that she would be back and that Miss Pugh must be ready to go.

In the alleyway we met Joe, and Beryl told him that Miss Pugh was still in the cabin and he swore and said that he would fetch her.

Now that it is all over and it has been in the papers and everyone wants to know about it, it seems foolish that I didn't understand. But Beryl did not sound afraid, just serious. There were noises and conversations in the alleyway but no rushing or raised voices.

The boat deck was crowded. The crew were launching lifeboats over the edge of the ship. It looked horrible — they were just going down into darkness.

They made women and children go forward and the men stood back. I did not want to go. Even then I did not understand that the ship was sinking. All I could do was be obedient and not move.

Some of the women would not get into the boats. They would not leave their husbands.

It was cold. We could see our breath. I think I heard music but maybe somebody only told me that later.

Some men were throwing the deck chairs over the rail, into the sea. I did not understand why.

Beryl was standing beside me, looking over her shoulder. Finally she said, "Come with me, then. We'll get in the boat together. No need to be frightened."

I said, "What about Miss Pugh?" but Beryl said that the captain wanted us to get into the boats as quickly as possible and that Joe would take care of Miss Pugh and they could get in a different boat. She took me firmly by the hand and led me forward. A crew member in charge loaded us into the boat and Beryl wrapped my blanket around me.

As the boat started jiggling down the side of the ship I finally knew what was happening. It was as though I woke up.

As we went down we passed bright decks with the portholes shining and then darkness. Bright and dark, bright and dark, bright and dark. There were even some people on the decks, looking ordinary.

Then a man slid down the ropes and landed in our boat with a crash. He was the one who was in charge and he said what we were all to do.

We landed in the water with a splash and some of the women in the boat cried out.

I knew I should have waited for Miss Pugh but I wanted to go with Beryl. I did not know who to be obedient to. I have wondered and wondered about what I did. I want to tell the truth now, in this record, but I do not know how to find it.

There were three men in the boat and they rowed. One had a face black with coal and he was wearing only trousers and a singlet until one of the women gave him a blanket.

The ship was bright. Way far away was another ship with lights and one of the men said we must row toward it and they would rescue us. They also said we must get away from the *Titanic*, for if it sunk it would suck us down. But I did not believe it would sink. You could not believe it. It was like saying a whole city was going to sink.

When you are having a dream it makes sense, like a story, but when you wake up sometimes you can only remember bits. Especially if it was a nightmare.

This is what it was like on our boat.

Beryl pulled the blanket around me. She tried to

hold me but she had on her lifebelt and so did I, so we could not get close. There was a baby on our boat. He began to cry when the boat hit the water. His mother tried to make him happy by playing peekaboo but he just cried on.

I put my head in Beryl's lap and closed my eyes. After a time there was a moan and I looked up and the lights on the ship had gone out. A minute or two later the ship upended and slid backward beneath the water. Somebody said, "She's gone."

Some people were praying.

One of the rowing men tried to get us to sing but we could not.

One more thing. I heard some people in the water. They were crying out for help. After a while I did not hear that any more.

My hand is too tired to write more. I will finish tomorrow.

June 23

Miss Caughey is smart about many things, but I do not believe that writing about the disaster is helpful. Last night I had the melting-face dream again. It is worse than ghosts or murderers or giant spiders or anything. Even the Jumblies ten times did not help.

June 24

I have been lonely before. When Charles moved away to the United States I used to go and stare into his room to try to conjure him home. When Mother and Father waved goodbye to me at the railway station and I was sitting in the carriage alone with Miss Pugh, I just wanted to curl into a ball. When Midnight died I kept thinking that I saw him, out of the corner of my eye. But I have never been so lonely as I was in that lifeboat. So lonely that there should be another word for it.

Beryl talked to me and told me that all would be well, and some of the other women were kind, but it was too cold and there was too much darkness all around. Too much darkness for the kindness to get through. The light of that other ship never seemed to get any closer. They were many stars. They only made me feel lonelier.

I could not stop my thoughts from sinking, down past one thin layer of wood to that water, black and cold and silent where a giant ship was sinking, sinking. I tried not to think of it, but it was as if my mind belonged to somebody else, or if I thought it through just one more time I could change what happened. I could keep the *Titanic* floating, huge and beautiful and lit up like a Christmas tree. If I thought of it just one more time, perhaps I could make it that we were simply on a lifeboat excursion so that we could see the whole ship, which we could not when she was in port, or certainly not when we were on it. But the story would not stick, so I would begin again, only to have it end with darkness, cold and silence.

Before the disaster I never really thought of the deep ocean beneath us. I did think about all the decks and all the rooms, with the fancy people all piled up, like layers in a cake, chocolate and raspberry jam and lemon curd and whipped cream. The ship was more like a big grand building than like a boat. I thought about the boilers and the engines but I never went deeper in my mind.

All night it was calm, but as the sky started to lighten, a breeze came up. When it was light enough to see, there were no other boats, just sea and ice. There were huge pieces of ice. First they were pink, then they turned gold as the sun came up. And that is when I made sense of all the talk of icebergs. That is what had happened. The *Titanic* had hit an iceberg.

In my mind, because I did not watch it disappear, I could not believe that it was gone. All those chairs and china and pillows and pianos and grapefruits. It was impossible. I did not think about all the people who had disappeared because I did not know that yet. The women who were crying for husbands and sons — I thought that they were on other lifeboats. I thought the people in the water would have been rescued.

As the boat began to move up and down in the waves, all my seasickness came back. I had to close my eyes and ears and think only of not being sick.

I was not sick, but other people were. The men were not rowing and nobody was talking. The only sound was the woman with the baby saying lullaby things, when one of the women suddenly pointed toward the horizon and there was a ship, first a dot, then getting closer. It was the *Carpathia.* All night Beryl had been cheerful and calm. When she saw the great ship coming toward us, so slowly, she said, "We're safe now," and she just began to sob.

June 25

What is underneath me? What is underneath me right now? What if I could dig straight down? Right now it is a mattress, bed, floor, corner of the dining room, floor, cellar, dirt, dirt, dirt.

Then what? The centre of the Earth. I remember talking about this with Grandfather.

I will pretend that it is breakfast at Mill House. I will finish this story by pretending that I am telling it to Grandfather and Grandmother.

The *Carpathia* came close to us and the rowing men rowed up against the side of it. There were lifeboats all around and many men's voices. There were ladders over the side. The two rowing men helped me into a seat like a garden swing and I was hauled up the side. It was like being pulled up a cliff. I would have been frightened but I had nothing left to be frightened with.

I had to use the toilet urgently and as soon as we were on board Beryl found one right away.

On the decks of the *Carpathia* everyone was milling around, looking for their people. I looked for Miss Pugh. Beryl looked for Joe. We did not find them. Beryl didn't leave me for a minute.

I found Marjorie and her mother right away. Marjorie was just saying, over and over, "Where's Papa? He said he was getting on that other boat."

I couldn't find the words to talk to Marjorie.

That is when I put together the things I had seen and heard.

There were not enough lifeboats for everybody.

Many people had drowned.

June 26

Everyone on the *Carpathia* was kind. The crew brought us food. The passengers shared their cabins. But they stared at us. This was the first of too much staring. That was the beginning of it.

When Irene accused me of liking all the attention, she was the exact total opposite of right.

People kept saying that other ships were in the area and some of them must have picked up more survivors.

We were three nights and four days on board. When I think of the five days on the *Titanic* I can remember what I did every hour, but the time on the other ship is blurry. Beryl found me some playing cards and I played Patience. She taught me Grandfather Clock Patience, which is more complicated than Clock Patience, which is what I knew. I made myself think that if I got it to come out three times in a row, then it would all not have happened. No iceberg, no sinking, no drowning. But I could not get it to come out three times in a row. If I got it to come out two times in a row, then there was another rescue ship sailing to New York with Miss Pugh, and Joe and Marjorie's father. But I could not get it to come out two times either, so I had to keep trying.

On the *Titanic,* Marjorie and I had mocked the people who just sat on deck chairs for hours, but that is what I did. Beryl brought me food. I was hungry all the time, hungry for cake.

I sat with Marjorie and her mother but it was like we had forgotten how to be friends, we had forgotten how to play.

Momon and Lolo were there, but not their father. There was a woman taking care of them. I had not seen her before.

The last day I did eat in the dining room, at a table with a woman with a baby. When lunch was over she took her dinner napkin and put it in her bag. She whispered to me that she had run out of clean nappies for her baby so she was making do. Nappies are the sort of thing that people in charge don't think about. I passed her mine as well.

Some kind ladies made space in their cabin and one of them took one of her own dresses and cut it down to make a frock for me. When she was sewing, her needle flicked in and out like a silver fish. I liked seeing her sew, but I did not like the frock. It stuck out. I should have been more grateful, but being grateful takes heart.

June 27

The time on board the *Carpathia* was a fog of cake and Patience. To help pass the time, Beryl told me stories. She spent the long hours telling me about when she was a little girl and all the places she had been and the ships she had been on and all the passengers she had served. The stories took me right away from worry and loneliness and the horribleness of wearing the same underclothes for five days.

Once when she was a stewardess on a Caribbean ship she went ashore in Jamaica with a friend. They wanted to get away from all the passengers and the hubbub of the port so they hired a driver and cart and went to a farther-away part of the island, near an inlet. Then they walked through the forest. By the time they got to the water it was getting dark and they were tired and hot so they decided to have a rest before they hiked back to the cart. They sat down on a log and chatted for a bit. Then there was a slurping sound and the log started to move. They jumped up and saw the great swish of a crocodile tail. They had been sitting on a crocodile's back! They ran like billy-oh back through the forest and when they got to the cart they were half-crying and half-laughing.

June 28

Hearing Beryl's stories on the *Carpathia* was comforting, but it is not so comforting to retell them. I need to get to that final day at sea.

We arrived in New York at night, in a cold rainy storm. We all went up on deck. As we approached the harbour there were lots of small boats with men shouting questions through megaphones and trying to take photographs with flashes of bright light. Beryl told me they were newspaper reporters. Someone called out to them to find out if there had been other rescue ships and they told us that *Carpathia* was the only one.

That is when I knew for sure that Miss Pugh had drowned. And Jack. And Joe. And Marjorie's father. And the quiet father of Momon and Lolo. But I knew already, because of the Patience. Beryl did not say anything. She just held my hand a little tighter.

Miss Pugh had drowned and it was my fault.

She did not get to the boat deck in time, and that was because she could not find her things and that was because I had thrown everything about the night before.

That is it. That is the truth I can tell only to these pages.

Miss Pugh was right. I am willful and wicked.

June 29

When you have done something terrible, it does no good at all to write about it. But I said that I would write the whole story so I will.

We left those small boats behind and people called out, "Get ready to see the lady!" They meant the Statue of Liberty. When she appeared in a flash of lightning everybody gasped. I didn't care about her; I only cared about who would meet me. Did Mother and Father know I was on the *Carpathia*? Did they know I was alive? Had they come to New York?

Beryl told me that she could not disembark with me because the crew had to get off last, but that there would be someone to meet me and take care of me and make sure that I got home safely. All that time on the *Carpathia* I did not cry. It was not that I was brave. It was like I was frozen inside. But when I had to leave Beryl I could not stop the tears. She gave me one tight hug and said that it was time to disembark via the aft gangway and now that I was a real sailor I was never to forget the proper names for things. I lost sight of Marjorie and I didn't get a chance to say goodbye.

There were wooden fences that made a path from the bottom of the gangway to the door of a big terminal because there were so many people waiting. They were waiting in silence.

As soon as I was inside the building, there was Charles. He didn't hug or kiss me. He just opened up his big coat and pulled me inside. It smelled like wet wool and tobacco smoke. It smelled like the safest place in the world.

June 30

When I finally got home after a train to Montreal and a train to Halifax and the horrible arrival with all those newspaper reporters, the first thing that Mother said to me was, "Oh, Dorothy, where did you get that dress?"

Two things about that moment. The first is that I remembered the care that Grandmother had taken so that I would not arrive home looking like a ragamuffin. She cut my hair and trimmed my fingernails. We even planned what I would wear on the day I arrived and she ironed a set of hair ribbons for me to wear when I left the ship. Then I arrived in a strange lumpy dress that didn't fit. I had scrapes and bruises on my legs that I didn't remember getting. I had been wearing the same underwear for five days. There were no hair ribbons.

The second thing is that I knew that Mother didn't really care about what dress I was wearing. She just said that because she didn't know what else to say. In plays people say real, important things every time they speak, but in real life sometimes words just fall out of your mouth.

July 1

White Rabbit.

I don't see the point of writing more except that I'm nearly at the end of the notebook.

Today we had a picnic for Dominion Day. Every year, old Mr. Thorpe next door gets up very early so that he can fly his flag at half-mast to protest Nova Scotia entering Confederation. This happened way back in the olden days but Father says some people have long memories and know how to hold a grudge. As we passed by his house he was out digging in his garden so I called out, "Happy Dominion Day, Mr. Thorpe." Mother shushed me because that was cheeky and forward but what she doesn't know is that Mr. Thorpe winked at me. I believe he waits all year for the pleasure of protesting and enjoys the holiday as much as any picnicking family.

Phoebe was at the picnic and she and Winnifred and I chummed around but they were talking mostly about something that happened at a basketball match this spring. Of course I wasn't there. I left them to it and went back to my family.

July 2

Jam. I have been chopping rhubarb. Mother is so patient when we are making something together. It is only when she is trying to teach me ladylike things and manners that I get so fidgety and cross. Sometimes I get so fidgety that I want to jump out of my skin, and all because she does something like lick her finger and run it across my eyebrows. I try to remember Mrs. Bland's advice on not staying cross one second longer than necessary, but it is easier said than done.

Mother asked me if I was feeling poorly and I said no and why did she ask and she said that I seemed a bit dreary. Then she said that she and Father had a surprise in store for me.

I'm curious as to the surprise but not really looking forward to it. I seem to have lost my taste for surprises. Maybe Mother is right and I am dreary. No wonder Phoebe and Winnifred don't really want to play with me.

July 3

Phoebe and her family visited this evening for a musicale. It all ended in a sad muddle. It was going along very well. I played "Camp of the Gypsies" on the piano without falling into disaster. Phoebe's sister Edwina played a complicated piano piece, one of those ones where you think the left hand must belong to an entirely different person than the right hand. If I practised scales night and day from now until I was twenty, I would never be able to play like that.

Then Father played a ragtime piece on the mandolin with much laughing and kidding from everybody. Then he said that Phoebe's father had to perform as well and Phoebe's father said he had no musical talents and Phoebe's mother said nonsense, he had a lovely bass voice and what about "Asleep in the Deep." Edwina started playing some chords and chivvying him so he finally started in on a sea song. He really does have a surprising voice, so deep and solid you feel you could stand on it. The song had a chorus that went like:

Many brave hearts are asleep in the deep
So beware.
Bee-ee-ee-ee-ware.

On the "ee" parts his voice went down and down and down. But just when he got to the final "ware" he happened to catch my eye and then he stopped singing and coughed and turned red and said, "Oh, I'm so sorry. Idiotic of me. I just didn't think."

And then everyone was embarrassed and didn't know what to do and still I didn't understand. Then I really thought about the words "asleep in the deep."

Oh. It means drowned.

I wanted to say something to make it all right, to get him to keep singing, to get everyone to keep laughing. I wanted to say, "I don't think about the *Titanic* every minute. It's not the most important thing about me. I don't want to be the reason to stop singing." But I couldn't say any of that and the musicale ended and then we ate cake and soon after that, people went home. I suppose the musicale was the surprise that was in store for me.

July 4

In stories it's the end when somebody comes home. In *The Railway Children* it ends when the father comes home from prison. In "The Jumblies" they all come back after twenty years away. But in real life things just go on. Now I'm not just myself but a "*Titanic* Survivor." This is like being a hero, but heroes are supposed to do brave things and I didn't do one brave thing. The only reason I am alive is luck, like a game of Patience.

July 5

The musicale was not the surprise!

I would write today as a play except that if I list the *dramatis personae* it will give away the surprise. So I'll just write it in the ordinary way. There is a lot to write so I'm not going to worry about perfect penmanship.

At breakfast Mother and Father were jumpy. Then Father had another cup of coffee, which he never does, and then he said he wasn't going to the bank but was taking the day off. Father never takes a day off, except for his annual holiday, which this wasn't. Then he said he was going out to fetch something. It was all very mysterious.

Later, I was up in my room making my bed and tidying when I heard him return to the house and then he called for me. When I got to the top of the stairs I saw him standing in the front hall with somebody wearing a large hat. Then the hat tipped back and it was Beryl!

I didn't run down the stairs. I flew.

Beryl was the surprise!

Mother appeared from the drawing-room and there were introductions and lots of adult talk. I found out that Mother and Father had written to Beryl. (They wrote to Beryl and didn't tell me? I did not have time to be angry.) First of all they wrote to thank her for taking care of me, and then asking her to please come visit any time she could and, by luck, she got a job on a ship stopping in Halifax and she has a day of shore leave and here she was and they so looked forward to getting to know her better but perhaps Dorothy would like to take her for a walk to the park first.

As soon as we were out the door Beryl started talking a mile a minute. She told me everything that had happened to her since the *Carpathia.* She told me that she was sorry that we did not get to say goodbye properly. She said that by the time the crew disembarked, the pier, which had been so crowded, was dark and empty. Then the crew was put in a tender to transport them to another pier, and from there onto another ship called the *Lapland* where they got to have dinner in the first-class dining room.

I remembered from the stops at Cherbourg and Queenstown that a tender is a smaller boat that delivers passengers and cargo to a ship. I was happy that Beryl was still treating me like a true sailor who uses the right words.

She told me that some of the crew had to stay in America in the hospital because they were sick and some of the crew had to stay to talk to important people about what went wrong on the *Titanic*, and why there were not enough lifeboats, but that she was allowed to sail home on the *Lapland* to Plymouth and from there she went to stay with her married sister. She said that her sister's children were like certain first-class passengers she could name and I would know what she meant.

I had forgotten how Beryl talks to me just as though I am her age.

Then she told me something amazing about the two little French boys, Momon and Lolo. Their father had kidnapped them and they were travelling under a false name! The father and the mother did not live together. I don't know why. They must have had a terrible fight or something. Beryl didn't know about that part. Anyway, the father kidnapped the boys and he was bringing them to America from France. He said his name was Hoffman but really it was Navratil.

After the disaster, the mother of the boys came from France to New York and took them home. I wonder if Momon still thinks it is funny to point to your knee and say "*Tête.*"

When we settled in on a bench in the park Beryl said that it was strange to go home. "They are always glad to see me, and gladder this time of course, but nothing really changes there." I said it was like when the Jumblies came home, and she didn't know about the Jumblies so I said the whole poem. She laughed and nodded and made me say the homecoming bit twice:

And in twenty years they all came back —
In twenty years or more:
And everyone said, "How tall they've grown!
For they've been to the Lakes, and the Torrible Zone,
And the hills of the Chankly Bore."

"The Torrible Zone," said Beryl. "That's a good description of what happened to us. We're Jumblies, you and I, because we've been to the Torrible Zone."

Then she told me that she had a big question to decide. A few years ago she was on a ship where she met an elderly rich couple from a place called Atlanta. They all liked each other. Beryl said, "They were complete dears." After the *Titanic* they read about Beryl and they found out how to write to her and they had written to offer her a job. Beryl said that they were offering lots of money, much more than she made as a ship's stewardess. And the work would be light. No more heavy trays. No more bells.

I'm going to copy what Beryl said next: "It will seem peculiar to say this, after that terrible night, but I fear I cannot do without the sea. A land job, even such a pleasant one as this, would seem tame."

She said that she cannot tell her sister about the offer because her sister would think she was "completely daft" to turn it down.

Then she asked me my opinion! I had to say that I didn't know. Secretly, what I was really wondering was if she had a sweetheart and if she was going to get married and have babies or if she was always going to make her own living, with or without the sea.

And then I had a new thought. Had Joe been her sweetheart? And because it was already so strange, sitting with Beryl on dry land, in Point Pleasant Park, I just asked her straight out. She smiled and said that no, he wasn't a beau but a true pal all the same and her heart was sore with missing him.

Then we sat in silence for a while and shared Beryl's hankie because I had left in a flurry without one (and without finishing making my bed or tidying my room either).

That is when it started to be like a play:

Scene: A summer morning. Point Pleasant Park, a bench.
Dramatis Personae: Beryl, a stewardess; Dorothy, a Canadian Girl.
Beryl, *takes off shoes:* Oof. New shoes and I haven't worn them in yet.
(Pause. Sound of waves lapping.)
Beryl: When my mind goes quiet I think about it.

(The CG does not have to ask what "it" is.)

Beryl: I go over the events of that night and try to make it come out different. I should have gone back for that Miss Pugh. I should have put you in the lifeboat and gone back. I think and think and I cannot imagine what went wrong, why she and Joe didn't come above deck, why Miss Pugh wasn't in one of the boats.
The CG, *confused. Beryl must have known that Miss Pugh was delayed because she couldn't find her shoes or her coat:* But . . .
Beryl: What?
The CG: It was my fault.

Beryl, *gives her head a little shake:* What?
The CG: The mess. I did it.
Beryl: What mess?
The CG: The mess in the cabin, when you came for us.
Beryl: There wasn't any mess.
The CG: But, I threw everything around, before I went to sleep.
Beryl, *frowns:* Oh. Is *that* what happened? I remember now. When I came into the cabin that evening, while Miss Pugh was at the hymn sing, things were a bit at sixes and sevens, so I tidied up, quiet-like because you were fast asleep. I was a bit surprised, now that I remember, because your cabin was usually quite orderly, not like some I could mention where it looked like a tornado had hit every day.
The CG: You tidied up?
Beryl: Yes, that was part of my routine.
The CG: Everything?
Beryl: Every bit.
The CG: But when you came for us, why was Miss Pugh saying, "Oh dear, where is this and where is that?"
Beryl: Because she was afraid. She was afraid and that made her even more dithery than

usual. She kept saying that she couldn't go above decks until she had taken the curlers out of her hair. I just did not feel I could wait. It was my responsibility to take care of you. But I do ask myself again and again, Should I have gone back?

CURTAIN.

That was when I started to feel dizzy.

There was no mess. Miss Pugh's coat was right where it should have been and so were her shoes.

There was no mess.

It was about curlers.

It wasn't my fault.

It wasn't my fault.

A gull swooped by at that moment, the sun shining off his wings. Then the sky was full of swooping, calling birds. Or maybe they had been there all the time.

July 6

I've done it. I've almost finished the notebook.

Beryl stayed all day yesterday. We scrambled about on the rocks at the park and then went home for lunch. Mother came with us to the Old Market. Beryl bought a basket. It was a day when everything seemed ordinary and funny. Aunt Hazel came for afternoon tea and Beryl told the story of sitting on the crocodile and another one about a pet armadillo and Aunt Hazel laughed so hard she inhaled tea up her nose.

Then Beryl asked Mother and Aunt Hazel whether she should go and live the easy life in Atlanta and I thought they would say, "Of course," but Aunt Hazel said, "No!" And Mother said, "A girl should make the most of life while she's young," which sounded almost like, **"A girl should make the most of life while she's young."**

Then Aunt Hazel looked at her watch and said, "Leslie will be home from the office by now. I have a good idea. Back in half an hour." When she returned she had Uncle Leslie and the Tudhope Torpedo. We all piled in and took Beryl down to the docks in style.

When we got there Aunt Hazel asked Beryl if she wasn't afraid to go on another steamship. "Not a bit," said Beryl, "I figure that I'm disaster-proof." Then she reached over and messed my hair. "That goes for Dorothy, too. She's a true sailor and, besides, what are the chances that she and I are going to be famous twice?"

I think that if Grandfather had been there he would have said that there was something wrong with Beryl's logic. But he wasn't, and standing there, on the tar-and-fish smelling, bustling dock, with messy hair, alongside a giant liner, and everybody smiling, it was the most perfect thing to hear.

Epilogue

Dorothy wanted nothing more than to put the *Titanic* disaster behind her. In some ways she succeeded. She refused all interviews. She did not attend reunions. The friends she made in later life had no idea that she was a *Titanic* survivor. She did not even tell her own children. It wasn't actually that hard to bury the past. Interest in the *Titanic* waned until mid-century. There was not a single non-fiction book published about the *Titanic* from 1913 until 1955.

For the people of Halifax, the sinking of the *Titanic* as a disaster story was trumped five years later when a French cargo ship loaded with explosives collided with another ship in Halifax Harbour, resulting in the world's largest man-made accidental explosion. Dorothy, in her final year at school, was at morning prayers when there was a huge crash and all the windows of the school were blown in. She was slightly injured. The school was turned into a hospital and many of the students spent the next few weeks in relief work. While distributing clothing to the homeless, Dorothy could not help remembering the kind women of the *Carpathia.* The following spring she wrote, for her school yearbook, a well-researched and heartwarming report on her experiences at the clothing distribution centre.

Following graduation, Dorothy went on to university. During her late teens she realized that, although she had tidied away her *Titanic* memories, her experiences during that spring of 1912 had left her with a fascination for news. The question of how the newspapers could have published such inaccurate information — "All Saved from *Titanic* After Collision" — continued to bother her. She left her studies before graduation and took a job with a newspaper, a move that worried her mother and delighted her grandmother. **("Absolutely what we need, women writing the news.")**

In the early days of her career, Dorothy was given assignments like editing recipes for date loaf or reporting on new styles of parasol. But as she proved herself to be an able writer, an energetic researcher and an effective interviewer, she was gradually accepted into the old boy's club of newspaper reporting and ended up as "Our Woman in Ottawa." She liked nothing better than debunking a myth or uncovering a scandal.

Beryl and Dorothy maintained a lifelong correspondence. Beryl did not take the job in Atlanta, but continued her career as a stewardess. Amazingly, she experienced a second sea disaster. In May 1915 she was employed on the Cunard liner *Lusitania* when it was torpedoed by a German U-boat and sank in eighteen minutes. She survived to spend the rest of her working life on the sea.

Owen went to university, supported by Dorothy's grandparents, and pursued a career in the British civil service. He was always very discreet about his actual job and Dorothy had a theory that he was a spy, but even with her skills at interviewing she never found out for sure. Millie married a young man from the village when he returned from serving in the Great War and they bought a confectionery and newsagent shop in London.

Interest in the *Titanic* was revived on the publication of a novel, *A Night to Remember,* in 1955, and even more so when a movie based on the book was made in 1958. Dorothy liked the book well enough ("enjoyable, for a novel," she pronounced) and she thought the movie was generally "well-researched and accurate," which were her terms of highest praise. But at the age of ninety-seven — in a wheelchair but still engaged with life — she could not be persuaded to go and see the blockbuster movie *Titanic,* even though her great-granddaughter, who had finally found out about her family's *Titanic* connection, begged her to. Dorothy declined. "I've seen the advertisements with that weedy little actor," she said, "and I just know that it is going to be **utter bilge."** So the great-granddaughter went without her. She did not find Leonardo DiCaprio weedy in the least.

Historical Note

A preschooler stuffs her Barbie doll into a yoghurt container and floats it around a plastic wading pool. The container tips over and begins to fill with water and sink. "*Titanic,*" shouts the preschooler.

Kids sit around a campfire and sing, with gusto:

It was sad, oh it was sad,
It was sad when the great ship went down
(to the bottom of the . . .)
Husbands and wives, little children lost their lives,
It was sad when the great ship went down.

Then the kids get sillier and sing:

Uncles and aunts, little children lost their pants.

An ebay auction advertises "an original piece of coal recovered from RMS *Titanic* during the 1994 expedition" but warns bidders that "the size of coal may vary."

The *Titanic* was not the only major marine disaster of its time. Two years later the *Empress of Ireland* collided with a freighter in the St. Lawrence River and sank, taking 1012 lives. The *Titanic* was not unique among luxury ocean liners. Her sister ship, the *Olympic*, was launched a year before her. Many lives were lost through natural disasters within a decade of the *Titanic*. Three thousand people died in the San Francisco earthquake and fire of 1906. Twenty-eight thousand people died in a volcanic eruption in the Caribbean in 1902. But it is the *Titanic* that everybody knows about. Why?

One reason that *Titanic* is a household word has to do with celebrity. Now, as then, we are fascinated with the lives of the rich and famous. A movie star has a bad hair day, a singer redecorates her bathroom, a celebrity spokesmodel ditches her boyfriend and suddenly the "news" is being tweeted and blogged and published in magazines. We are hungry for details. The *Titanic* had, among her first-class passengers, a wide selection of the 1912 equivalents of rock stars. Some of the travellers, such as the Countess of Rothes and Sir Cosmo and Lady Duff Gordon, had titles. Some were known for their accomplishments. There was an aviator, a sculptor, an artist, a moviemaker and a best-selling writer. What really caught the public's interest, however, was wealth. John Jacob Astor, Benjamin Guggenheim, George Widener — these were the super-rich, the names that everybody knew, that filled the public with that mixture of fascination and envy that celebrity creates. The combined wealth of the first-class passengers is estimated to have been $9.8 billion in today's dollars. Their clothes, their jewels, their pets, their cars, their toys, their hanky-panky (Mr. Guggenheim was travelling with a woman who was not his wife) — buckets of newspaper ink were spilled, and continue to be spilled, on such details.

The fascination of sunken treasure is another reason we continue to wonder about the *Titanic*. What's left of that magnificent liner lies 3798 metres under water. All that luxury, all that history just waiting to be discovered. Plans to raise the *Titanic* started very soon after the disaster. One of the goofiest ideas involved filling it with ping-pong balls in order to refloat it. The trouble with all these plans was that nobody knew where it was. Expeditions in 1980, 1981 and 1983 failed to find the wreck, but in 1985 a video camera surveying the ocean floor in the area of the disaster began to pick up a trail of debris that led to the ship. The man who first saw it, Robert Ballard, described it as "an apparently endless slab of black steel."

Some questions were answered with the discovery. Several survivors had said that the ship broke in two as it sank, and the wreck confirmed that to be true. Some items were salvaged in later years, including bits of coal, but it is unlikely that the wreck itself will ever be raised. It remains a memorial. It keeps its secrets.

The *Titanic* disaster also continues to engage our imagination because it leaves so many questions and mysteries. Separating rumour from fact has been a century-long pastime. Did Captain Smith rescue a baby? Was there an Egyptian mummy on board that cursed the voyage? Did some ship's worker paint *We defy God to sink her* on the stern of the ship?

The disaster also raised more serious questions. At the time people asked, How could the "unsinkable" *Titanic* sink in less than three hours? Why were there insufficient lifeboats? Why had there been no lifeboat drill? Why didn't the *Californian*, a ship in the vicinity of the tragedy, respond to the *Titanic*'s signals for help? Who was responsible?

People wanted somebody to blame and they wanted there to be a meaning in the disaster. For some people that meaning was the danger and wickedness of new technology. In St. Matthew's Church in Halifax on Sunday, April 21, 1912, the Rev. J.W. Macmillan preached: "We must fix the blame upon ourselves for the crime of a generation, reckless in its pursuit of a debauch of pleasure, and these sixteen hundred victims are hapless sufferers.

Our society today is like a band of children in a storehouse of dangerous tools and explosives and playing games with gunpowder, matches, steam and electricity in a reckless and wanton fashion."

Looking back from the perspective of our times, one of the questions that the *Titanic* raised was the huge moral issue of the value of a particular human life. The world of the *Titanic* was rigidly divided into classes, based on wealth. A first-class ticket cost an average of $480 and third-class passage cost an average of $35 — that works out to over $11,000 for a first-class ticket and about $800 for third-class, in today's dollars. The first-class passengers had access to the Moorish-tiled Turkish baths and the third-class passengers shared two bathtubs among seven hundred people. Did anybody question these divisions? Probably not. Everyone was warm, dry, well-fed and experiencing one of the wonders of the age.

But then the *Titanic* struck an iceberg. There was space for 1178 people on the lifeboats and there were approximately 2200 people on board. Who gets saved? The unwritten rule was women and children first. The men who stood aside as those women and children were loaded into the lifeboats were memorialized as heroes.

Another Halifax preacher on that Sunday said, "It is a lesson of love that it is indeed self-sacrifice which is at the heart of all heroic life." Others weren't quite so sure. A reporter in the *Halifax Morning Chronicle* wrote: "John Jacob Astor, Master of millions, Chas. M. Hayes, Railway Magnate, and the rest stood aside for sabot-shod, shawl-enshrouded, illiterate and penniless peasant women of Europe." Is the life of a captain of industry worth more than the life of an ordinary, unnamed immigrant woman? The reporter seems to have his doubts. The survival statistics tell one version of the story. Sixty-three percent of first-class passengers were eventually saved, forty-three percent of second-class passengers and twenty-five percent of third.

Who deserves to live? What decision would you have made? What would you have done on that cold, crowded and confusing boat deck?

One hundred years after the luxury liner *Titanic* sank to the ocean's depths, it is still news. It was not until 2007, for example, that the identity of the "unknown child," buried with such ceremony in Fairview Cemetery in Halifax, was revealed through DNA testing. He was Sidney Leslie Goodwin, aged nineteen months, travelling in third class. His parents, two sisters and three brothers all perished in the disaster.

The *Titanic* lives on because it is the best of stories. It has exotic luxury, arrogance, greed, mystery, heroism, self-sacrifice, romance, suspense, vibrant characters, the implacable forces of nature, the power and ingenuity of huge machines and, at its heart, a little empty space, a space just big enough for us. In our private *Titanic* story are we a baronness or a lift boy, a second officer or a penniless peasant woman of Europe? Or maybe we play in the orchestra. Maybe we are one of the stokers who stayed too long in the pub in Southampton and missed the maiden voyage. At the end, maybe we were safely packed onto a lifeboat, or we jumped into the frigid water in desperation or we sat in the first-class lounge and played cards while the ship went down. In our private story, be our theme tragedy, irony or luck, the one thing we never are is ordinary.

* * *

Dorothy and her family, in Halifax and in England, are all fictional characters. Their world, however, includes some real historical people. Mrs. Bland, who wrote under the name E. Nesbit, was a real writer and her stories are still great fun to read. *Titanic* passengers Momon, Lolo and their father really existed. Captain Smith was indeed the captain of the *Titanic*. Fred the lift boy was also a real person, Frederick Allen, age seventeen. He did not survive.

The Titanic *sails from Southampton on April 10, 1912. When the* Titanic *was launched she was the largest man-made moving object in the world.*

This cross-section image of the Titanic *shows the locations of the first-class room* (D), and *the third-class cabins* (E).

staterooms (A) *and dining room* (B), *the second-class staterooms* (C) *and dining*

The Titanic's *maiden voyage was to be Captain E.J. Smith's last command before he retired.*

A woman tries out one of the exercise bicycles in the Titanic's *well-equipped gymnasium..*

R.M.S *TITANIC*

APRIL 14, 1912.

DINNER

CONSOMMÉ TAPIOCA

BAKED HADDOCK, SHARP SAUCE

CURRIED CHICKEN & RICE

SPRING LAMB, MINT SAUCE

ROAST TURKEY, CRANBERRY SAUCE

GREEN PEAS PUREED TURNIPS

BOILED RICE

BOILED & ROASTED POTATOES

PLUM PUDDING

WINE JELLY COCOANUT SANDWICH

AMERICAN ICE CREAM

NUTS ASSORTED

FRESH FRUIT

CHEESE BISCUITS

COFFEE

A facsimile of the dinner menu, served in the second-class dining saloon the night the Titanic *struck the iceberg, includes the delightful-sounding "American ice cream" and the not-so-delightful "pureed turnips."*

In this artist's recreation we see lifeboats being lowered the 22 metres (75 feet) from the boat deck to the water as other boats, already launched, pull away.

A lifeboat carrying Titanic *survivors, photographed as it approached the rescue ship* Carpathia. *A note on the back indicates it might have been carrying the "Nairatil" [Navratil] children.* *See photo next page.*

Two French brothers, Michel (4) and Edmond Navratil (2), survived the sinking of the Titanic. *Their father, who was taking them to America without his wife's knowledge, died.*

Passengers on board the Carpathia *improvised clothing for the* Titanic *survivors from blankets and their own clothes.*

Headlines around the world trumpeted the Titanic's *sinking. Some early editions wrongly reported that the ship did not sink and was being towed to port. The sinking of the* Titanic *was the greatest news story of its age.*

Coffins and hearses line the dock at Halifax, waiting for bodies to be unloaded from the cable ship Minia, *which helped the* Mackay-Bennett *recover bodies. The Mayflower Curling Rink in Halifax served as a temporary morgue, where families of the victims could identify the bodies and recover their possessions.*

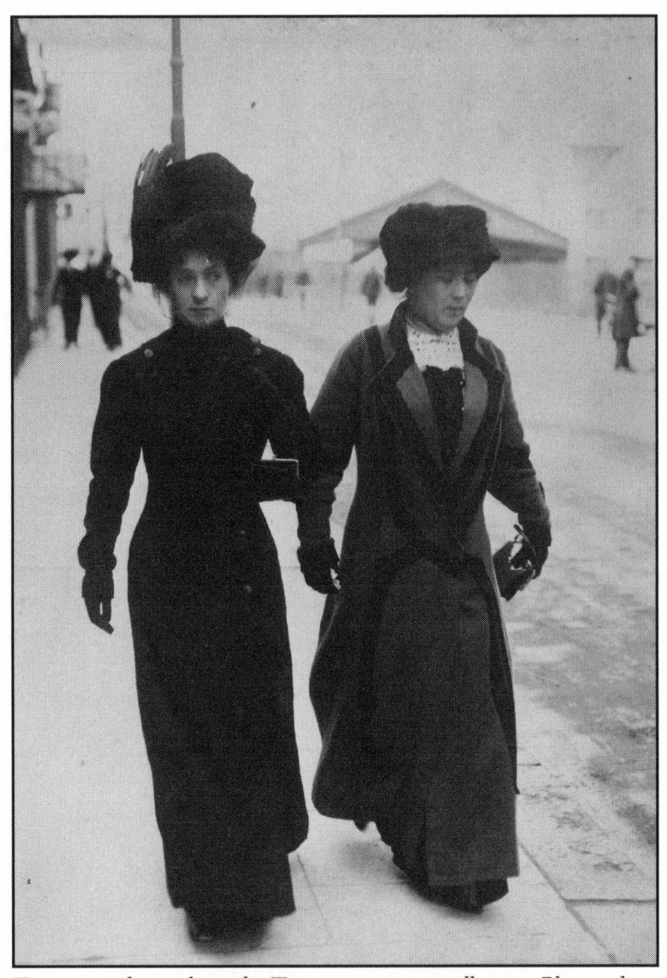

Two stewardesses from the Titanic *are seen walking in Plymouth, upon their safe return after the disaster.*

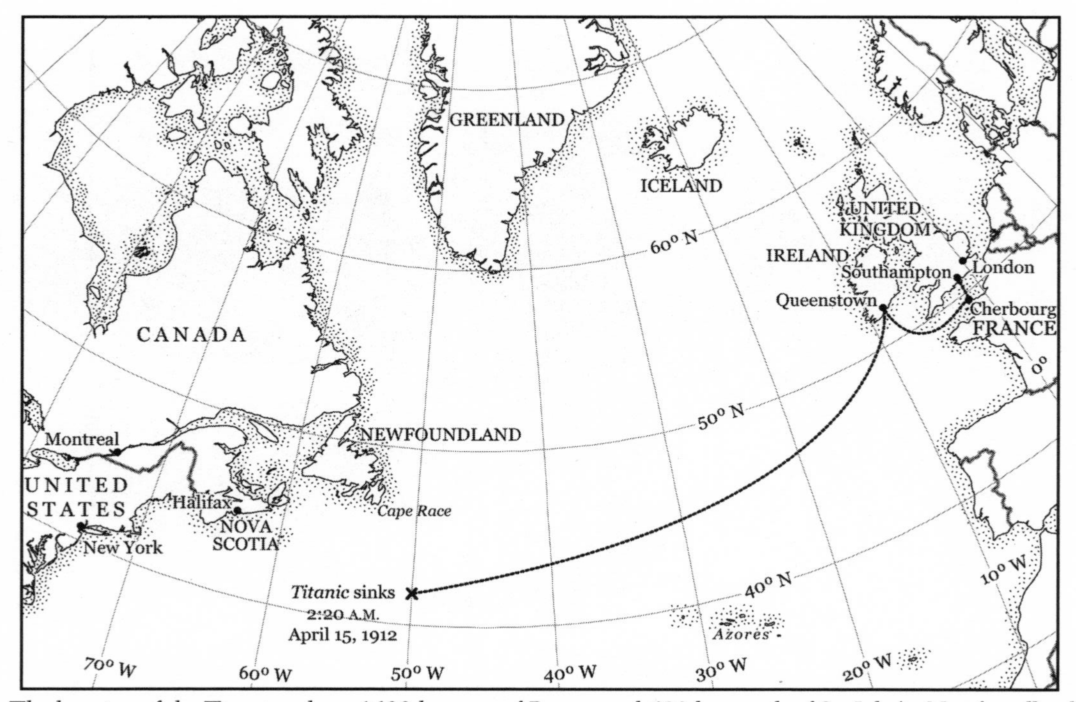

The location of the Titanic, *about 1600 km east of Boston and 600 km south of St. John's, Newfoundland.*

Acknowledgments

Grateful acknowledgment is made for permission to reprint the following.

Cover cameo: Detail, *Young War Worker,* Getty Images/Keystone, HGE:2666206.
Cover background: Detail, painting by Ken Marschall © 1982.

Page 149: *Titanic*, Brown Brothers PIX 428.
Pages 150-151: *CROSS-SECTION OF TITANIC. The White Star liner that sank, April 14-15, 1912, after having struck an iceberg in the North Atlantic while on her maiden voyage,* image no. 0061041, The Granger Collection, New York.
Page 152: Southampton City Council Arts & Heritage.
Page 153: *TITANIC: GYMNASIUM, 1912. A passenger keeps fit aboard the* "Titanic," image no. 0074265, The Granger Collection, New York.
Page 154: From the *Titanic*'s second-class dinner menu, April 14, 1912.
Page 155: *THE 'TITANIC,' 1912. The lowering of the lifeboats on the White Star liner* "Titanic" *after she had struck an iceberg in the North-Atlantic on April 14, 1912;* contemporary illustration, image no. 0046019, The Granger Collection, New York.
Page 156: Photograph of a lifeboat carrying *Titanic* survivors, National Archives and Records Administration, ARC identifier 278338 / MRL number 383.
Page 157: *TITANIC: SURVIVORS, 1912. Two French brothers, Michel (age 4) and Edmond Navratil (age 2), who survived the sinking of the RMS* 'Titanic;' *their father died in the disaster, and at the time of this photograph they had yet to be returned to their mother.* Photographed April 1912, image no. 0109464, The Granger Collection, New York.
Page 158: TITANIC. *Succouring the saved: Women passengers on the* "Carpathia" *sewing for the* "Titanic" *survivors and distributing clothes,* image no. 0005882, The Granger Collection, New York.
Page 159: Newspaper boy, Express Newspapers, ©topham Picturepoint, Getstock.com 2225800159.

Page 160: *Hearses lined up on Halifax wharf, near present jetty 4 in HMCS Dockyard to take R.M.S.* Titanic *victims recovered by C.S.* Minia, *6 May 1912;* NSARM Photograph Collection: Transportation & Communication: Ships & Shipping: R.M.S. Titanic #3, Nova Scotia Arms and Records Management.
Page 161: Southampton City Council Arts & Heritage.
Page 162: Map by Paul Heersink/Paperglyphs.

The publisher would like to thank George Behe of Encyclopedia Titanica for his expert commentary on the text, and Barbara Hehner for checking additional details.

For Carmen and Winnie

Author's Note

When I was doing the background reading for my story of Dorothy and the *Titanic* I felt as though I were swimming in a sea of facts. The *Titanic* disaster is one of those subjects that lends itself to facts, the *Guinness Book of World Records* kinds of facts. There is even a word for people who become fascinated with these facts — Titaniacs, as in "maniacs." For a time I became a Titaniac. How many ostrich plumes were in the cargo of the ship? What pieces did the orchestra play? What was the value of the diamonds on board? How tall, how big, how rich, how many, how far, how fast? My friends were patient as I regaled them with fact after *Titanic* fact.

As I started to write my story, however, I found that the facts were not as inspiring as the images, the stories and the might-have-beens. For example, on April 17, 1912, the cable steamer *Mackay-Bennett* left Halifax Harbour to search for bodies from the *Titanic*. (Nine-day search, 306 bodies, 116 buried at sea.) It must have been a gruesome and traumatic job for the sailors, the embalmers, the undertaker and the clergyman. The image that stayed with me came from a newspaper description of the wharf as the steamer was being prepared to leave. The reporter talks of the usual hustle and bustle of the port. At the inner end of the pier is a pile of a hundred coffins. Halfway down the pier are big blocks of ice being transferred to the ship's hold, and at the far end of the pier is a crowd of reporters with their cameras. The ice was to preserve the bodies they found until they could return them to Halifax for identification and burial. I couldn't include this scene in my story because Dorothy was not there to see it, but the irony of the image has haunted me: Loading ice into a ship to go out into an ice-filled sea.

The big story of the *Titanic* is like a collage of microstories. Here's one: When survivors in the lifeboats first saw the rockets that the rescue ship *Carpathia* (3:30 a.m., Cunard Line, 743 passengers from New York heading for a Mediterranean cruise, travelling at top speed of 17.5 knots toward the survivors) was firing, they signalled to them by burning newspapers, personal letters and handkerchiefs. My storytelling brain wonders about this. Who takes a newspaper on board a lifeboat? More seriously, what about those letters? What letter would be so important that you would stuff it in your pocket when your ship was sinking? And what about burning it? Would you have a moment's hesitation? Of all the things you own, what would be the one thing you would grab when the fire alarm rings out, when the flood waters are rising, when the ground begins to tremble beneath your feet?

Any story of a disaster is a story of might-have-beens, a chain of alternating fortunates and unfortunates. Twenty-two-year-old Kit Buckley had a ticket to travel from Ireland to Boston on the *Cymeric,* a small ship of the White Star line in the spring of 1912. Unfortunately, there was a coal miners strike and the liner could not sail. Fortunately, she was rebooked on the *Titanic.* Unfortunately she was a third-class passenger and perished, body number 299. Further unfortunately, her family blamed her half sister for encouraging her to travel to the new world. This casting of blame caused a bitter family rift. Fortunately, nearly one hundred years later, the two parts of the family were finally reconciled in a ceremony in which they erected a headstone on Kit's grave.

Our best photographs of life aboard the *Titanic* come from the lens of an Irish theological student, Francis M. Browne. Browne was fortunate enough to have been given a first-class ticket for an overnight passage on the *Titanic* from Southampton to Queenstown. Huge and impressive machinery, scenes of action, elegant people — what an opportunity for a keen photographer! He spent the afternoon of the departure day and the next morning taking pictures. How unfortunate that he was only to be on the ship for two days. Fortunately, he made friends with a millionaire couple on board who took a shine to him and offered to buy him a ticket all the way to New York and back. Unfortunately, when Father Browne cabled his superior to ask for permission for the longer trip the answer was clear: "GET OFF THAT SHIP." Fortunately, Francis Browne obeyed the order and thus survived — only 17 percent of males in first class survived, so his chances would have been slim. His amazing photographs also survived; they are the last visual record we have of life on board the great ship.

Even more intriguing than the might-have-beens are the might-not-have-beens. Because of the *Titanic*, Canadian writer Linda Bailey might never have been. Her grandmother, who emigrated from Poland in 1912, was supposed to travel on the *Titanic*, but family plans changed at the last minute. As Linda says, "They were peasants, so we know where my grandmother would have ended up." Next time you enjoy one of Linda's Good Time Travel Agency books you are only two clicks away from the night when the great ship went down.

The web of connections to that fatal night fans out across many countries, from three-year-old French Haitian Simonne Laroche to Mr. Mauritz Håkan Björnström-Steffansson, a businessman from Sweden. In third class: Mrs. Mary Sophie Halaut Abrahim from Lebanon. In second class: Mrs. Anna Hamalainen from Finland, travelling to join her husband in Detroit. In first class: Doña Fermina Oliva y Ocana, from Madrid, travelling as a personal maid. A French musician, a fireman from Hong Kong, an American governess — these were some of the survivors. How many lives did they touch in the years following the disaster?

And then there are the ghosts — "Died in the sinking. Body not recovered." Ilia Stoytcheff, age nineteen; Alfred Peacock, age seven months; Telda Marilda Strom, age two; Houssein Mohamed Hassan Abilmona, age eleven; Jeannie LeFebvre, age eight. What would have happened to them in the new world that was their destination?

The original *Titanic* was built of steel (overlapping plates 3 cm thick) and rivets (three million of them) at the Harland and Wolff shipyards in Belfast, Ireland, by over fifteen thousand workers. It took fourteen months to build. It is now located approximately 1600 km due east of Boston and 600 km southeast of St. John's, Newfoundland, about 3798 metres below the surface.

Our *Titanic*, on the other hand, the *Titanic* for the twenty-first century, is made of stories, of biography and history, of the ghost stories of the might-have-beens, of my fictional story of Dorothy Wilton. This *Titanic* is located north, south, east and west of our fascination. This *Titanic* is still under construction.

* * *

Sarah Ellis won the Governor General's Award for *Pick-Up Sticks*, and has twice been a finalist. She has also won the Mr. Christie's Book Award, the IODE Violet Downey Award, the Vicky Metcalf Award for Body of Work, the Sheila Egoff Award and the TD Canadian Children's Literature Award. She has written over a dozen books, including *A Prairie as Wide as the Sea, Days of Toil and Tears, The Baby Project, Back of Beyond, Big Ben, The Queen's Feet* and *Odd Man Out.* She lectures on children's literature, teaches creative writing, and contributes reviews to a number of publications.

While the events described and some of the characters in this book may be based on actual historical events and real people, Dorothy Wilton is a fictional character created by the author, and her diary is a work of fiction.

www.scholastic.ca

Library and Archives Canada Cataloguing in Publication

Ellis, Sarah
That fatal night : the Titanic diary of Dorothy Wilton / Sarah Ellis.

(Dear Canada)
ISBN 978-0-545-98073-9

1. Titanic (Steamship)--Juvenile fiction. I. Title. II. Series: Dear Canada

PS8559.L57T54 2011 jC813'.54 C2011-902616-3

7 6 5 4 3 Printed in Canada 114 17 18 19 20 21

The display type was set in Bolton Sans.
The text was set in Goudy Old Style.

First printing September 2011

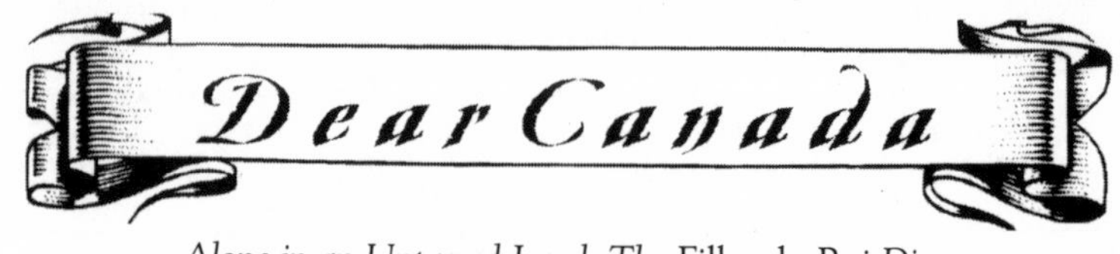

Alone in an Untamed Land, The Filles du Roi *Diary of Hélène St. Onge* by Maxine Trottier

Banished from Our Home, The Acadian Diary of Angélique Richard by Sharon Stewart

Blood Upon Our Land, The North West Resistance Diary of Josephine Bouvier by Maxine Trottier

Brothers Far from Home, The World War I Diary of Eliza Bates by Jean Little

A Christmas to Remember, Tales of Comfort and Joy

Days of Toil and Tears, The Child Labour Diary of Flora Rutherford by Sarah Ellis

The Death of My Country, The Plains of Abraham Diary of Geneviève Aubuchon by Maxine Trottier

A Desperate Road to Freedom, The Underground Railroad Diary of Julia May Jackson by Karleen Bradford

Exiles from the War, The War Guests Diary of Charlotte Mary Twiss by Jean Little

Footsteps in the Snow, The Red River Diary of Isobel Scott by Carol Matas

Hoping for Home, Stories of Arrival

If I Die Before I Wake, The Flu Epidemic Diary of Fiona Macgregor by Jean Little

No Safe Harbour, The Halifax Explosion Diary of Charlotte Blackburn by Julie Lawson

Not a Nickel to Spare, The Great Depression Diary of Sally Cohen by Perry Nodelman

An Ocean Apart, The Gold Mountain Diary of Chin Mei-ling by Gillian Chan

Orphan at My Door, The Home Child Diary of Victoria Cope by Jean Little

A Prairie as Wide as the Sea, The Immigrant Diary of Ivy Weatherall by Sarah Ellis

Prisoners in the Promised Land, The Ukrainian Internment Diary of Anya Soloniuk by Marsha Forchuk Skrypuch

A Rebel's Daughter, The 1837 Rebellion Diary of Arabella Stevenson by Janet Lunn

A Ribbon of Shining Steel, The Railway Diary of Kate Cameron by Julie Lawson

A Season for Miracles, Twelve Tales of Christmas

To Stand On My Own, The Polio Epidemic Diary of Noreen Robertson by Barbara Haworth-Attard

A Trail of Broken Dreams, The Gold Rush Diary of Harriet Palmer by Barbara Haworth-Attard

Turned Away, The World War II Diary of Devorah Bernstein by Carol Matas

Where the River Takes Me, The Hudson's Bay Company Diary of Jenna Sinclair by Julie Lawson

Whispers of War, The War of 1812 Diary of Susanna Merritt by Kit Pearson

Winter of Peril, The Newfoundland Diary of Sophie Loveridge by Jan Andrews

With Nothing But Our Courage, The Loyalist Diary of Mary MacDonald by Karleen Bradford